DARK SHADOWS

Ann Thorsson

Typeset in Sabon

Editing, typesetting and publishing by UK Book Publishing

www.ukbookpublishing.com

ISBN: 978-1-915338-14-3

To Henriette.

My No. 1 fan and stalker...

Other books by Ann Thorsson

A gritty drama set in the 1980s coal mining North of England. This is no ordinary boy-meets-girl Romeo and Juliet. (pub. 2019)

Can be read as the prequel to *Dark Shadows*.

"'Downhill' is endearing and scary, sweet and disturbing, all at the same time.

...we get to love the characters and wish their lives wouldn't take certain directions. To me, only a well written and powerful book can do that."

Matt Ferraz, Author. (Five-star review)

Ann Thorsson
DARK
DREAMS

How long can Maggie run and hide before the
truth catches up with her?

A dark and disturbing tale of secrets and lies, with a supernatural twist. (pub. 2020)

"From the beautifully crafted sentences to the simple but powerful ingredients, Thorsson turns the words into a film playing in your mind. She knows how to make the characters jump off the page!"

Lisa G Shannen, Freelance Writer and Author.

Prologue

Have you ever felt like
you're being watched or followed?
That goosebumps, skin-crawling
sense of someone close-by...

You don't want to look over your shoulder,
or look out of the window
because you know their eyes are upon you.
Eyes watching your every move.

Turning around could bring you
face to face with your stalker.
That person who's making your life
HELL...

Chapter 1

Homecoming

Monday 27th July, 2015

Alana stood and looked at the cottage while she waited for the taxi driver to retrieve her bags out of the boot. Though it had been quite a few years since she was last here, it still looked as neat and smart as the day she had walked down the front path and away from her life in the countryside.

Away from Jack.

Away from her marriage.

Away from all that was burdening her psyche.

Moving to yet another fresh start, this time in the city; a place where she could blend in, and lose herself in the crowd. A place where she could focus on herself and her writing.

She and Jack had chanced upon the cottage – or cottages, as it was back then – while out for a countryside drive, just as the estate agent was putting up the "for sale" sign. Woodend Cottages were a pair of old, stone-built farm workers' cottages, "ripe for modernisation" according to the agent's sales details. Tangled old ivy had become intrinsically woven into the front elevation, while the two huge stone chimney stacks, one on each gable end, looked like metaphoric strong arms and shoulders embracing the cottages. Youthful energy and creative vision meant they just had to buy it.

Months of drawing up plans and waiting for permissions, followed by hard, intense work, finally saw the two cottages knocked into one and renamed in the singular, to Woodend Cottage. Even Jack's connections as an architect couldn't make things move any faster. More months of interior remodelling and decorating had given them the cosy home of their dreams. The renovations had been a clichéd labour of love; a peaceful haven where she could write by day, and snuggle up with her hubby at night in front of the woodburning stove. Both of the tall chimneys had been retained for this very purpose, meaning they could install an Aga in the dining kitchen, and create a stone Inglenook fireplace for the woodburner in the sitting room. Weekends had been given over to developing the garden, or scouring antique fairs and farm sales for all the right pieces to create the overall look.

But in every fairytale, there's a wicked witch. An antagonist to spoil the idyll. Alana's wicked witch was her mental health. And like all wicked witches, the bitch found more ways than one to sneak up on her victim and offer poisoned apples. One by one, the metaphoric poisoned apples had taken her down; worn away her resolve until she cracked, and cracked again. And there are only so many times that you can crack before the shattered pieces can't be put back together again. In her case, it was her marriage.

The city had proven to be a large, noisy, welcome diversion to all that had been torturing her mind. An anonymous respite from years of intense darkness. A vibrant distraction away from the dark shadows.

Yet here she was: back at her old marital home for a month on a self-imposed writer's retreat to finish *Brutal Honesty*, her fifth novel. So why now? And why here, of all places? Because it was once again time to face old ghosts. And this place was as good as any to sneak in under the radar and face them.

Alana walked slowly up the gravel path, her stomach pricked by nervous curiosity. The paintwork to the window frames and front door looked neat and fresh. The gardens looked well-tended, and the cotoneaster had all but covered the faded scars in the stonework to the right hand side, where they'd taken out a door and replaced it with a window. But then again, this kind of holiday cottage, particularly in this area of the Peak District, commanded premium rental prices – they had to look the part. Talking of "looking the part", what would the cottage look like inside? Jack's new wife, Olivia, was an interior designer, so Alana was pretty sure that she would have maximised and capitalised on the cosy country-style look. Hopefully not all rose-prints and horse-brasses…

She fumbled in her handbag for her notebook. The cottage now had a security alarm system – a standard requirement these days, particularly on rental properties in this area. She found the page with the code-numbers for the key-box and alarm. Both numbers were the same – 2902 – the leap-year date. Should be easy enough to remember. But then again, she was highly unlikely to set the alarm for the duration of her stay. Too much faffing around. Alana punched in the code to the key-box to retrieve the keys.

After disarming the alarm system, the first thing that Alana noticed was the lemony, lingering smell of furniture polish and surface cleaner as she entered the cottage. She briefly wondered whether Olivia employed someone to do the cleaning, or if she did it all herself. Alana smirked as she tried to envisage Ms Elegant pushing a vacuum cleaner around and changing the beds after every Airbnb booking. It somehow didn't fit her style.

Still pumped by curiosity, Alana carefully placed her luggage in the hallway and took herself on a tour of her old home, closely inspecting each room. Mercifully, the cottage seemed to have escaped the "country-twee" overkill. In fact, it was simple yet tastefully furnished and decorated. Some pieces of furniture she recognised; quality pieces that had been retained after the divorce. Other items were new, but still looked the part. Alana conceded the fact that Olivia had good taste.

She headed for the kitchen to make a pot of tea before unpacking her things, grateful to see that they had thoughtfully left her a little basket of essentials on the kitchen table, and a carton of milk in the fridge. A little handwritten welcome-note was humorously tucked into a hand of bananas:

"Hi Alana!

Welcome back to Woodend. Please don't hesitate to get in touch with us if there's anything that you need. You have our phone numbers.

Best wishes,

Olivia & Jack xx"

Alana studied the beautifully scripted handwriting, all swirly and girly. Definitely not Jack's scrawl. Her stomach fluttered, as doubt began to niggle at her. Would she be able to settle into writing at the cottage for a month? Would it be like slipping on a pair of comfy old shoes? Could she cope with seeing Jack and Olivia together?

Or would she be plagued by old memories and old feelings?

Chapter 2

Getting Organised

Tuesday 28th July, 2015

Energised by her morning jog around the lanes and post-jog shower, Alana sat at the kitchen table with a newly-made pot of tea, a fresh mind, and her ever-present pad of sticky notes ready to make a plan for the day. She had to concede, it was much nicer taking a run in the countryside than pounding the city streets. Timing her regular morning run before the roads filled with car fumes and the pavements became congested with blinkered commuters was essential, otherwise the point of taking daily exercise was counterproductive. She poured herself a cup, and absently tapped the top of her pen between her teeth while she allowed her thoughts to formulate. Shopping – that was a definite. While the little welcome basket provided by Jack and Olivia had been a great arrival-day stop-gap, the fridge and cupboards needed to be stocked with enough food and milk to last for at least a week. That way, she could have a heads-down writing focus without intermittent distractions. Next on the list, train times for tomorrow's excursion – this would be the *only* distraction that she would allow herself. Alana added writing and editing to her list, and made a note to take a serious look at chapter fifteen. There was something about this chapter that didn't flow with the rest of the storyline, and needed to be re-written.

She removed the towel from her head and rubbed the ends of her hair before giving her head a shake. A few droplets of water landed on her pad of sticky notes, causing dark circles of dampness. The word "Shopping" began blurring and spreading. Alana rolled her eyes and tore off the top few pages until she reached a section of dryness. She started a new list:

*Run
*Shower
*Shopping
*Train times
*Writing & editing (esp. Ch.15)

She immediately crossed through the already-completed top two tasks on her list, thereby giving herself an instant sense of achievement. Was there anything else that she needed to do today? Her mind scanned across other potential jobs – the writing area on the dining table had already been set up with the printer and pack of A4 paper, notebook, sticky notes and pen-pot... Nope, all good. She peeled off the to-do list and carefully stuck it down on the kitchen table.

Next list – her shopping. Alana mentally walked the aisles of Sainsbury's (although she was pretty sure that everything would have been moved around since she last shopped there). That said, she would only be able to buy as much as she could carry home, so would have to shop wisely with light but versatile ingredients. Maybe pop into the nearby High Peak Bookstore and get a few books to read for evening relaxation? Always good to see what other local authors were writing. Assured that her life was now all in order for the day, Alana gave herself a satisfactory nod, then ran her fingers through her now-drying hair and mussed up the ends, careful not to dampen her sticky notes again.

Time to get on with things!

* * *

Alana's assumption of the aisles having been swapped around since her last visit to the supermarket proved correct. Nothing was where she remembered. It would make her shopping trip take longer than anticipated, but there was nothing she could do to change it. List in hand, Alana took a deep breath and forced herself to relax. Most of her shopping would be found in the chiller-cabinets, so she headed in that direction. Items like fresh pasta, and salad would be light and easy to carry back to the cottage, and being a seasoned "cooking for one" type shopper, she had learned how to maximise use-by dates, and mix-and-match choices.

Her train of thought and focus was interrupted by her phone ringing. She reached into the back pocket of her jeans to retrieve it, apologising to the shopper by her side for the intrusion. It was Jack. Alana exhaled loudly with an exasperated *ugh*. She felt sorely tempted to ignore her ex's call, but politeness prevailed.

'Hi, Jack.'

'Hey, Alana! Welcome back... How was your trip?'

'Just fine. No hitches, or delays.' She continued browsing the chiller, unable to decide between the mozzarella and basil stuffed pasta, or the Mediterranean tomato. She checked the length of the use-by dates, then dropped both packs into her basket. 'And thanks for the little box of stuff, by the way. It was really useful. It meant that I could just spend the rest of the day settling in, without having to rush down to the shops.'

'That's what we thought.'

Alana took note of the *we*.

'Anyway,' Jack continued, 'we wondered if you'd like to come over to our place this evening for dinner. Save you having to cook just for one.'

Alana rolled her eyes. Going for dinner to her ex's house, and being fawned over by wife #2 while she showed off her culinary talents was not something which Alana wanted to take part in. Nor did she fancy having to listen to his golf-club stories, or do the ubiquitous grand-tour of their perfect showhouse barn conversion, he being an architect, and her an interior designer...

'Thanks for the invitation, Jack. That's really kind of you. No offence, but I'm going to decline. I really want to settle into my writing rhythm. After all, that's what I'm here for. I'm sure you understand...' She heard Jack sigh into the phone.

'Well, if you're sure. You'll be missing out on feta and olive stuffed avocado, salmon, and squidgy chocolate brownies...' he teased.

'Tempting,' she laughed. 'But, no. I'll pass, thanks. Like I said, I just want to get into the flow, and get this project wrapped up. I'm on a deadline – and if anyone should appreciate the pressure of a deadline, then I'm sure you two can,' she quipped. Alana purposefully omitted to tell Jack that she would be taking a trip out tomorrow. It would only rake up old arguments.

'Ah, yes – the deadly deadline! Okay, that's a fair enough excuse. Anyway, I'd better get back to it – I'm also on a deadline. You have my number if you change your mind, or if there's anything that you need.'

'Thanks, Jack. Bye for now.'

'Bye, Al–'

Alana swiped to end the call before her ex had finished speaking. She sighed and took a deep breath. Ah, yes – tomorrow's trip. She needed to stop by at the florist...

Chapter 3

The Pilgrimage

Wednesday 29th July, 2015

Three generations of the same family: grandmother, father, and son, made their way along the gravel pathway of the cemetery towards the gated exit; the son linking arms with his father, who in turn was linked to his own elderly mother, helping her to navigate the uneven surface. Their tones were hushed and appropriate for the location, none wishing to raise their voices for fear of waking the dead. Let them sleep in eternal peace.

Three generations of the same family who had come to pay their respects: to a brother who had passed too soon; to a mother who had died of a broken heart, and to a grandfather who was no longer in pain.

Will hugged his father close. 'I can't believe it's been twenty-five years since we lost our Jon... It feels like only yesterday that we were playing together in the garden, and messing around in the sand pit.' He sighed, the weight of losing his twin brother still laying heavy on his soul.

'I know, lad. The pain and memory still cuts deep wi'me, too. Even though the years peel away little layers of grief, the heart of the grief never seems to fade. But that's how it should be – remember them for who they were.' Ged shivered in the unseasonably cold July weather; weather not too dissimilar to the day they had laid Jon to rest. The breeze ruffled his silver-grey ponytail. He might now be in his early fifties, but he still couldn't let go of his long hair. He'd already had to let go of so much of his past... Somehow, his hair, and Will, felt like all he had left. 'C'mon, let's get back to the hotel and get warmed up. Y'gran's half frozen.'

As Will helped his father put Gran into the back seat of the car, his eye caught sight of a woman in the Children's Garden of Rest. He watched as she made her way among the graves towards a plot he knew well – the grave of his twin brother.

'I'll be back in a minute, Dad. I think I've dropped my wallet. It probably fell out while we were laying the flowers...'

He slipped back into the graveyard, and made his way to the gateway which led into the Children's area, enabling him to watch the woman from behind the neatly clipped privet hedging without her seeing him. The woman looked around, as if checking to make sure she was alone. She then stood at the foot of Jon's grave with her head bowed low, before stooping to place a single white rose at the foot of the guardian angel headstone. After what looked like a moment of prayer, or some kind of contemplation, she blew a little kiss, then stood up and began walking towards the exit. Will quickly stepped back, shielding himself behind a nearby weeping willow tree.

There was something about the woman which seemed familiar to him. Will racked his brain to try and make some kind of connection, before snapping his fingers in realisation. It might have been twenty five years ago since he last saw the woman's face, but now the white roses that they'd found over the years made sense. A kaleidoscope of emotions tore through him as he recalled the moment of his brother's death: one moment they were playing in the sandbox, the next, hearing a dull thud and screams. Watching as his parents ran from the house, his mother screaming hysterically...

He remembered his father shielding him from the tragedy unfolding before their eyes.

He remembered the shriek and wail of the ambulance, mixed with the shriek and wail of his mother.

He remembered seeing the face of the young woman in the passenger seat of the car which had hit Jon; her face rigid with shock, fear and disbelief.

His family were not the only ones paying an annual pilgrimage to his brother's grave.

Elaine McCairn was also making an annual visit to the cemetery in Castle Ridge.

Mind's Eye

I am four...

"It's here that I recall some of my earliest childhood memories...

Nature or nurture? This question has been debated by experts for years. Maybe it's the early years of being nurtured that develops our nature and personality? Who knows?

For me, these early memories are painful. In my mind's eye, I can still hear their fights and arguments. They hated being my parents – I was the unexpected consequence of a boozy night and a fumbled shag in a dimly lit alleyway.

As a small child, I was very introverted. I never went to playschool, so I had to find my own entertainment – mostly my colouring book and wax crayons. It gave me some escape into another world. And it was while I was sat colouring that I used to listen in on their arguments...

I would hear things like, "I should have gotten rid of it..." (I was classed as "it", not "her"), or "I should never have married you – I was forced into doing the right thing...". Though I didn't understand the meaning of their words back then, somehow they stuck with me. And it's very painful once you realise the definition of their reluctance to be responsible parents. Elaine, the unwanted and unloved.

Booze was their poison and their priority. If they could get to the pub, then they were happy. They very often used to go out together, particularly at weekends, and leave me home alone. I *think this is one of the reasons that I was such a nervous child, and developed a fear of the dark. Luckily, one of the neighbours saw them out together one night and gave them a really good telling off – and threatened to report them to Child Services. So after that, they would argue over whose turn it was to go to the pub, and I would be piggy-in-the-middle. Neither of them wanted to stay home and take care of me. And even when they were home, they just slumped in front of the TV with a few bottles or cans of beer.*

I liked watching telly, too – especially the animal programmes. My favourite programme was Animal Magic, with Johnny Morris. He used to make funny voices for the animals and make them sound like they were talking. It made me laugh. And Play School – that was another fun programme. I used to love guessing which window we'd go through. Or trying to work out the time on the clock, then guessing what the story would be about from the clue-figure beneath. Innocent escapism.

Luckily for me, I was about to start Infants school – a new and exciting chapter in my life. I couldn't wait to go, and really looked forward to learning lots of new things. I especially wanted to learn how to read and write! I looked forward to getting out of the house and away from their filth. When you've watched sit-coms on TV with "happy families" laughing and having fun, you soon realise that you're not one of them.

Little did I realise that I had no real social skills or social norms to be among other kids..."

Chapter 4

No. 1 Fan

Thursday 30th July, 2015

He scrabbled around in the semi-darkness, the bushes and foliage snagging on his matted hair and beard, grabbing at him like bony old fingers. Damp earth and stones irritated his knees through the thin cloth of his piss-ridden trousers. He found a comfortable spot where he could hunker down and watch Alana, unseen; refocusing the binoculars directly into the sitting room, the French doors affording him a great view. The farmer's loss was his gain, the day that he found the binoculars lying around in the old hay barn. It brought him visually closer to Alana, even when he couldn't get physically close.

It was nice to see Alana back in Derbyshire – she'd been away for too long. After her divorce, she had moved to Manchester, making it almost impossible to watch her. He did try, but kept getting moved on for being a "scruffy old beggar", or looking like a tramp. No-one wanted to look at his unkempt appearance, or smell his unwashed smell. His only option had been to leave the city and return to the safety of the countryside.

Try to put her out of his mind.

He had caught sight of her jogging down the lane early yesterday morning, much like she used to do when she lived here. After waking in the old barn, he'd taken his usual track into the woods to use the little stream for his morning ablutions. He might be a free-walker, but he still liked to splash water on his face every day, and enjoy a stroll in the fresh morning air. And there she was.

A very old flame, rekindled.

She looked quite a bit different to when he remembered her from the early days. Classy. Time had been kind to her. And she had set a career-path for herself along which he could never really follow. He was grateful for that.

His path had taken him to dark places. It had left him no choice but to move from town to town, jobbing for cash until he had gotten the sack – usually for turning up drunk. Hostels and soup kitchens had become his daily warmth and sustenance, until even they had closed down through lack of charitable funding.

Then one day, he had chanced upon Alana – or rather, a poster of Alana, in a newsagent's window, advertising an upcoming book-signing "tour" of local bookshops. He recognised her straight away, even with the different name. He knew full-well that he wouldn't be able to go into the shops, but at least he could follow along and watch her from the shadows. That would be enough. After a few weeks of lurking and following, he finally figured out where she lived. Luckily for him, there was a farm nearby with a cosy barn in which he could sleep at night – providing he slipped in once it had gone dark, and left before the farm buzzed into life. This had become his new abode, and he had been careful to remain unseen; an evanescent part of the landscape in which he lived.

And now here he was, back in the garden of the woman he loved – a love that would never be reciprocated, but, hey-ho. At least she had come back to the cottage alone; there didn't appear to be a "significant other" in tow.

The heady fragrance from a nearby rose bush filled the evening air. He closed his eyes and steadily inhaled the sweet perfume. Memories of a mis-spent life were briefly set to one side. In his mind, it was just him and his girl.

A rose.

He would give her a red rose...

Chapter 5

Afraid of the Dark

Friday 31st July, 2015

Satisfied with her day of writing and editing, Alana clicked on the little printer icon, then selected the pages she wanted to print. Today had been *extremely* productive – almost 4,000 words. They had quite literally flowed out of her imagination to her fingers. However, this brought with it painful writerly consequences: stinging, watery eyes, stiff fingers, and even stiffer shoulders. Sitting at the dining table was not the best place to work; the dining chairs were hard and upright. They might look fancy, but they were anything but practical. Her brain felt like gloopy pink blancmange – a feeling she usually got prior to a migraine, and a definite indicator of too much screen-time. The printer shook as it churned out the precious pages. Even though her manuscript was auto-saved in Drive, Alana had a deep distrust of the cloud-system. Surely there would come a day when the cloud would burst, overloaded with all the world's data? A digital catastrophe of global proportions, and a catastrophe she did not want to be a part of. It had taken her long enough to make the transition from using Word and USB back-ups for her writing. Old dog, new tricks, and all that.

Alana logged out of her account then closed the lid of her laptop, before rolling her shoulders and tipping her head from side to side. The taut muscles in her neck pinged in protest as she stretched, causing sharp stabbing pains. A loud sigh escaped involuntarily – a sigh that meant she had to stand up and go to the French doors to close the curtains. She caught sight of her own reflection in the glass and hesitated. A wave of nervous energy moved up from her stomach and tied a knot in her throat – surely any external observer would see the same? Maybe if she turned off the lights first, then whoever was out there wouldn't be able to see inside…

'Oh, for fuck's sake, stop being such an old woman!'

Spurred on by the volume and conviction of her own voice, Alana took control of her nervousness, first turning off her work-lamp before flicking off the main light. She waited a moment for her eyes to adjust to the semi-darkness before heading over to the double doors, carefully navigating the furniture en-route – the throb of last night's bumped shin still a fresh reminder of the room's layout. Coffee tables were a particular death trap. Some of the furniture had been moved around since she had moved out of the cottage, plus there were some new additions. All very irritating. Why did things need to be changed? But then again, Jack and Olivia were well within their rights to do as they wished – it was *their* place now; no longer hers and Jack's.

Alana felt reassured by the weight of her mobile phone in the top pocket of her shirt – a rectangular shield of defence should the need arise.

The penetrating darkness beyond the safety of the glass felt oppressive. Deep, yet strangely inspiring. There was something about this dark tension that was seeping its way into her writing – her own experiences were being transported into her latest novel; all that she felt, her protagonist felt. It was psychologically cleansing to offload this daily tension onto someone else, albeit a fictional character. Personal trauma and people-watching provided literary embellishment for most authors.

It put the juicy meat onto the bones of an otherwise bare storyline.

She mulled over her current situation – it calculated like the clichéd stereotypical formula of a psychological thriller: lone female + remote cottage + rising tension + dark night = predictable outcome. Alana snorted to herself at her overly-dramatic thoughts. Why not throw in a power cut, a thunderstorm, and an escaped axe murderer for good measure! Muahahaha...

And yet here she was, slap-bang in the middle of this self-same predictable storyline – a lone female booked into a remote(ish) cottage for a month. A writer's retreat; a hideaway with the minimum of distractions, under pressure from her agent to get her arse in gear. The all-important deadline lurked in the recesses, like a predatory animal waiting to pounce on its unwary prey. If nothing else, staying at the cottage would help to keep her butterfly-mind focused, away from the buzz of city life.

Alana narrowed her eyes as she scanned the expanse of deep shadows for any sign of movement beyond the lawn. But it was impossible to determine who or what was out there; the vague moonlight barely illuminated the garden. Every bush looked like a crouching person, every tree a grotesquely distorted figure. How could such a (normally) picturesque view appear so malevolent in the absence of daylight? Particularly as it was a view she knew well – a garden that she had tended and nurtured over the years. She had taken it from a weed-infested and overgrown mess into a glorious mix of herbaceous borders, shrubs and cottage wildflowers: cornflowers, poppies, tall hollyhocks, and fragrant rose bushes. Trees had been carefully pruned and pollarded to give them a new lease of life.

She checked that the French doors were locked and bolted, only to check twice more – just to be sure – before pulling together the heavy curtains, eager to block out the night. The countryside was one of those places that looked picture-postcard idyllic in daylight, or under a blanket of soft, freshly fallen snow. But in the absence of street lighting, the darkness felt like the fathomless depths of Hell.

Yet Alana sensed – knew – that someone was paying her unwelcome and unwanted interest. She had experienced a similar sensation the day before yesterday when she had visited the graveyard, although that felt more like ghosts from the past watching her every move. But finding a red rose on the front doorstep this morning, tied with a hand-written note on a dirty, torn piece of cardboard, from her "No. 1 Fan"... And a rose from the cottage garden, at that! Well, that had sent her mind into overdrive.

Jack had denied all knowledge of it being from him when she called him. But then again, why would her ex-husband leave a stolen rose on the doorstep? Who, then? She wasn't exactly one of the BIG authors; not quite up there with the literary giants, yet well-enough known for people to nudge elbows in the local supermarket, or stop her to say how much they enjoyed her work. A *minor* celebrity, if she were to pin a description on her literary success.

But this...

This oppression lurking in the dark shadows.

This stress-induced knot in the stomach.

This prickling of the scalp.

This constant feeling of being watched.

The fear was real.

And it was out there.

Chapter 6

Life Imitating Literature

Saturday 1st August, 2015

Wispy fingers of low-lying mist, gently illuminated by the early morning sun, seeped across the stubbled cornfields, creating an ethereal, glowing blanket across the land. The farmer hid in the shadows; his posture as straight as the trees in which he was stalking his prey. He prided himself on being furtive; elusive and unseen. His ever-watchful eyes were sharp, his senses keen and tuned into the land; keeping tabs on all movement, either in the trees or on the ground. His shotgun was cracked, carefully hung over his forearm. Dappled camouflage from the sunlight and trees provided the perfect cover for him to skulk around the woodland. A flash of movement caught his eyes, as Alana jogged down the lane, seemingly oblivious that she was now being watched.

He blinked in surprise as she stopped then suddenly vanished below the hedge-line, only to pop-up again a few paces later. She repeated this strange movement a couple of times, before looking around then continuing her journey. Curiosity ignited, he focused his new binoculars to get a better look. These binos were much better than the old ones...

It was her again, the woman from the cottage. He'd noticed her a couple of times this week while on her morning jog. He absently mused over the many times that he'd watched her before she'd moved away. She was just as lean now as when she used to live here. Maybe her hair was slightly longer, scraped back into a pony-tail. He noticed how it danced seductively from side to side in time with her jogging steps. She used to jog up and down the lane back then, or cycle. A blush rose to his cheeks causing a rush of warmth, as he recalled the occasion when he'd inadvertently zoomed in on her backside with the binoculars while he was patrolling the top acres. He knew that it was wrong to look, and in all fairness he'd been scanning across the fields watching some hares chasing around when she'd cycled into view.

Some nearby pheasants broke through his reverie, their deep, throaty clicking sounds bringing him back to the present moment. He mentally chastised himself for his lapse in concentration – those were the birds that he should be watching, not a bit of old totty jogging down the lane. He checked his watch: 7:30 am. Time to head back to the farmhouse and the cooked breakfast that would be waiting for him.

I must remember to tell the missus that that writer-woman is back at the cottage... I'm pretty sure she'd like to take her some eggs or a pie – find out what she's doin' back here...

The muddy brown colour of the free-walker's overcoat afforded him the perfect camouflage as he crouched behind the hedgerow. A chuckle rose in his throat as he watched Alana from his vantage point. What a fun little game he'd organised for her this morning! A paper-chase! Bobbing up and down as she gathered up the pieces. She did look a little cross, though. Or was that fear in her eyes? He hadn't meant to frighten her, just have a bit of a laugh.

Maybe she was still cross about finding the rose yesterday morning? She certainly didn't look very happy when she opened the front door and almost stepped on it. Not the look he'd hoped for. He sighed –

perhaps she'd recognised it as one of the cottage garden roses? And yet it had been given as a genuine gesture of affection. He'd even tried to add a little humour on the tag – after all, he was still her number one fan. Maybe not from a reader-perspective (although he did have a couple of her books), but definitely as an admirer. He'd done his best, under the circumstances.

It had been interesting rummaging through her dustbin – you can learn so much about a person from their rubbish. Luckily for him, Alana had thrown away some stale bread, mercifully not yet mouldy, though a little dry. A welcome addition to the freshly-picked wild blackberries.

The torn-up paper made for exciting reading – little snippets from her story-writing. He could understand why her books were popular – she was certainly good with words.

That's when he hit on the idea to scatter the paper and make a trail. He could guide her slowly along the lane and have a more lingering view of her. It was tempting to lead her right to him, but...

***

The heat of the water and the calming fragrance from the shower gel seeped into Alana's psyche. She could feel the tension in her muscles slowly easing, and her core beginning to relax. Steam rose into the air and rolled over the top of the curtain rail, like an autumn fog creeping over the top of a mountain ridge. The shower was her thinking place; a place where she could calmly, and without distractions, set her mind going for the day. A place where many of her writing ideas could be formulated before sitting down at her laptop and letting them escape onto the page.

But this morning was different. Her mind was being tormented by the recent strange occurrences: first was the unnerving feeling of being watched from the garden, then the red rose which she had found on the doorstep yesterday morning. Perhaps it had been genuinely left there by someone who liked her work, and who knew that she was at the cottage? She was, after all, well known in the local area. Many of the townsfolk had acknowledged her in the supermarket, or spoken to her on the high street since she'd arrived back a few days ago. She couldn't exactly be holed up for a month without going out for her daily run, or without picking up supplies, even if she was trying to maintain focus. Life still had to go on around the writing. Alana tried to think of all the people with whom she had casually chatted while out and about. Could any one of those be the culprit?

And then this morning's contribution was finding the wheelie-bin tipped over, surrounded by food packaging, and a scattered paper trail down the path and lane. Paper which she recognised as being edited scraps from her torn-up manuscript. All very strange. It had made her morning run to the bakery and newsagents all the more nerve-wracking, not knowing if someone was going to jump out from the hedgerows. Perhaps it was a fox? Perhaps it was the same person who had left the rose? Either way, it was all becoming a little too sinister – the stay at the cottage was meant to be a restful retreat. It had left her with no choice – she would have to call Jack and get him to come over. Maybe ask him to improve the security lighting. Something had to be done! Alana shuddered, then turned off the shower. Perhaps a leisurely breakfast with the freshly baked croissants and coffee, and the weekend newspapers would help to calm her nerves? She allowed herself the luxury of a few quiet moments to listen, before pulling back the curtain.

This was the downside to being a crime writer – everyone became a potential suspect, and every room a crime scene...

Mind's Eye

I am six...

"Another one of my earliest memories, and one that still haunts me to this day, is peeing my pants in class – it was one of those Portacabin classrooms at Castle Ridge Infants School. The teacher was reading a story to us, and we were all sitting on the floor, listening. Story time was such an escape for me – it took me to another time, another world, another existence. I was so engrossed in the story that I didn't want to miss a word, nor did I want to interrupt the teacher. She was such a storyteller, with a voice that kept children rapt with attention. And so I sat there and peed my pants instead of asking to go to the loo. Besides which, going to the loo meant going outside to the block of toilets in the playground – there were no toilets in the Portacabin, you see. As you can imagine, I wasn't very popular with the teacher when she realised why the kids were making a commotion. There was a little pool of warm yellow liquid around me that was slowly growing larger. She was the one who had to clean it up, of course. And typically, I didn't have any spare clothing with me. I didn't really have that many clothes, anyway. I was the smelly kid in class who no-one wanted to sit next to – that pissy kind of smell when you haven't changed your knickers for a week. It must have hung like a toxic cloud around me. But that's just how it was – clean clothes on a Monday, and I had to do my best to keep them clean for the rest of the week. I knew that I stunk to high heaven – I could smell it on myself. Looking back, I'm surprised that the teachers never reported it to the authorities. Yep, I learned at a very young age to have low self-esteem...

Another memory, again at Castle Ridge Infants School, was during one lunch playtime – it was a frosty autumn day, and I was wearing ankle socks. Yes, ankle socks! Well, you should have heard the dinner lady who was on duty – she went nuts. I was one of those kids who liked to hold the dinner lady's hand and walk and chat. I didn't really have a choice because none of the other kids wanted to play with me. She was a kindly old lady – you know the ones – they have nothing better to do with their day, so they do volunteer work at school as dinner ladies. Anyway, she wasn't happy with my mother, let me tell you! Fancy sending a young child to school in ankle socks when it was so cold... It was nice to have someone stand up for me.

But what could I do? My very presence got in the way of home life – I was the constant source of their arguments.

Whose turn was it to look after me so that the other one could go out to the local pub?

Whose turn was it to look after me so that the other one could go to bingo?

And then they'd start fighting, and I'd be piggy-in-the middle. Hiding under the dining table became my safe zone.

I was the kid that nobody wanted.

Nourishment, such as it was, followed a predictable routine for each day of the week. All of it boiled to death and overcooked into some kind of tasteless slop, or deep fried and dripping with grease. And that's if she could be bothered to cook – the chippie, or microwaved pasties from the corner shop were a regular alternative. Thank goodness for school meals – at least I had one good meal per day.

It was no wonder that I used to wet the bed. Which was probably another reason why I used to smell so pissy. And just because I'd wet the bed didn't mean that my bedding got washed and changed regularly. Nope. A tatty old towel would be folded up and laid over the wet patch. In the end, my mattress developed a hole in the middle, it was so rotten. Yes, really!

All I ever wanted was to feel loved.

To feel cared about.

It's not a lot to ask for, when you're six..."

Chapter 7

Conundrums

Sunday 2nd August, 2015

'**B**ingo! *That's* who she is!'

Since returning home to Skegness, following the family's visit to the graveyard in Castle Ridge, Will couldn't get the face of Elaine McCairn out of his mind. Though he had peeled back the years and recognised her as the passenger in the car which killed his twin brother, there was something else about her face that had been *recently* familiar. The lightbulb moment had finally arrived after hours of searching the internet. Although he had struggled to find anything about Elaine McCairn after a certain point in time, he had finally made a connection; the search had revealed a name change.

He thought back to the moment a couple of days ago when he saw her standing by Jon's grave. Over the years in which the family had visited, they had occasionally found a single, fresh white rose already laid at the foot of the headstone. White for purity, he guessed. The gesture had often puzzled them, but they had put it down to others who had remembered Jon. He had been such a likeable little lad.

Curious to know more about her, he continued his search under the new name. He found that she had a website, and social media pages. Time to dig deeper into the life of Alana McQueen, novelist; author of crime thrillers.

As he read through her website biography, Will learned that she had successfully published four novels, and was currently residing in the Peak District while putting the finishing touches to her fifth. Link-clicks began taking him on an internet journey into her alter-ego; her life history unfolding before him. Pictures of Alana with her books at book fairs, author-signings in local shops, samples of her work, promotional photos of the local area in which she had lived; all moments of pride. Being a hobby-writer and poet himself, Will appreciated the hard work behind the pen.

He looked deeper at the beautiful countryside in the various photo-backgrounds and realised that he recognised some of the places: the iconic glass dome of Buxton's Pavillion Gardens, Solomon's Temple standing proud atop Grin Low, the entrance to the caves at Poole's Cavern; places that his dad had taken him when he was much younger. Even though he had lived in Skegness since being a young boy, Will had never thought of it as "being on permanent holiday". When the holiday-makers came in, the locals went out and became tourists elsewhere. For Will and his dad, it was usually back to their birthplace of Castle Ridge and the surrounding Peak District. Despite all the years of living in a different county, Derbyshire still held a special place in their hearts.

Yet there was something behind Alana's smile that suggested sadness. Maybe it was the pain of that day in July 1990 which still haunted her.

He scratched his head and rubbed at his chin; his unshaven stubble making a rasping sound. Surely if she had been visiting the graveside for the past twenty-five years, she must still feel deeply about the tragedy? He pondered for a moment while he considered his next move. Maybe he should acknowledge her gesture in some way? After all, it was quite heart-warming to see that she still cared; that she hadn't just walked away from what had happened.

'Here, I brought you a cuppa... She's pretty. Who's that?'

Will jumped at the sound of his father's voice behind him, Ged having entered the office unheard. Feeling like a teenager being caught watching porn, a blush rose to his cheeks, his father's unexpected entry leaving him no time to fumble on the keyboard and minimise the pages he had open.

'It's, erm, it's an author that I'm browsing...' fluffed Will.

Ged homed in for a closer look as he carefully set the mug of tea on the desk beside the computer screen. Will had chided him many times for putting liquids too near the keyboard. He squinted at the text, before drawing away sharply. Now it was Ged's turn to feel flustered. He took a few moments to recompose himself before speaking.

'I suppose you've figured out who she is, then?'

Will nodded, and sighed before replying. 'I'm sorry, Dad. I didn't mean to rake up old memories, or open old wounds... I saw her the other day when we were at the cemetery. She's the one who's been leaving the white rose on our Jon's grave all these years. I saw her do it.' He hung his head, not wanting to make eye contact with his father.

'You don't have to feel bad about this, Will. I had a sneaking suspicion that it was Elaine leaving the roses... Poor woman – she was practically hounded out of Castle Ridge. Her and her boyfriend were made scapegoats for something that was an accident.'

'Well, at least she's gone on to better things – look...' Will flicked back to one of the other tabs which showed Elaine's – or rather Alana's, author website. 'She went on to become a successful writer. According to the web-blog, she's back in Derbyshire at the moment, putting the final touches to her next novel. I presume she used the opportunity to visit the cemetery...'

'So she changed her name? I don't blame her.' Ged pulled up a chair and sat beside Will. 'I'm glad that things worked out okay for her in the end. I wonder what happened to her boyfriend, Steve?' He pondered a moment, as if searching for a memory. 'I never blamed them for anything – I hope you realise that, Will...'. He looked at his son, his eyes seeking Will's approval.

'I know you didn't, Dad.'

'Thanks.' Ged cleared his throat while he tried to find the right words. 'You know there's a rift between me and yer Nanna Jean? Well, that's because of all this gossip. After Jon died, she was always on the side of those laying the blame with Elaine and Steve. Once Elaine had left Castle Ridge, the rumours subsided. Anyway, after yer Mam died, the gossip machine fired up again. There was this one day, I was helping out at Nanna Jean's veg shop, lifting some bags of spuds into the back. Well, I heard her saying some bad things about Elaine to one of her customers, connected to your Mam dying... Gossip that sounded similar to when our Jon had died. So I confronted her about it. As you can imagine, it caused a right bust-up between us. That's another one of the reasons why I decided to sell the cottage, and move us to Skeggie. I just couldn't be a part of her bitterness. It's like she'd forgotten all the bad things that y'Mam had done to me...' Ged exhaled loudly. 'As much as I loved her, yer Mam was no saint...'. He looked at the white scar across his palm; a faded reminder of the day that Julie had deliberately burned his hand with red-hot curling tongs. Retribution for having lost his job. His eyes began filling with tears. 'Sorry, lad – I didn't mean to rake up old ghosts...'

'Hey, you didn't – it was me, remember. I started this by trying to find out who this woman was at the graveyard. And as morbid as it might seem, I'm glad that she still feels a connection to that day. It's obviously still painful for her, too.'

'Aye, you're right. But – we can't change what happened. All we can do is remember them, and move on.' Ged squeezed his eyes with his fingers to push away the moisture that was building, and stood up. 'Anyroad, I'm going to make a fresh pot of tea. Do y'want a top up?'

'Erm, yes, please. I'll come through in a minute – there's just one more thing that I want to do.'

Will opened another tab on his computer to search for florists which had a delivery service in the Peak area.

Chapter 8

A Game of Two Wives

Sunday 2nd August, 2015

Still rattled by his visit to see Alana, Jack shook the rain from his Barbour coat before hanging it up in the wet room. Having been summoned to the cottage by his neurotic ex, he would now have to face a grilling by Olivia. Not a full-on "drag-him-over-the-coals" grilling, but that underground "current-wife versus ex-wife" kind of surreptitious questioning. He took a deep breath and prepared his best poker-face before heading through to the kitchen. With his hair still dripping wet and plastered to his face, he hoped that Olivia would be more pitying than curious.

Olivia looked at Jack, her eyes wide – partially with concern, but mostly because of the water-trail that he was leaving in his wake. Realising his soggy mistake, Jack quickly retreated to the wet-room to grab a towel for his hair.

Though she felt like raging at him for going out in the bad weather at the beck-and-call of his ex, Olivia knew how to play the questioning game. Showing compassion brought better results and answers – a Game of two sides. She similarly played her poker-face to hide her fury.

'So, how was Alana? Did you manage to sort things out for her?' she asked.

Jack shook his head by way of reply, causing droplets of water to splash onto the island countertop. He sat down on a barstool and poured himself a core-warming coffee from the freshly prepared cafetière.

'Not really. She still seems obsessed with finding that red rose on her doorstep a couple of days ago. It's really shaken her up. She just can't seem to accept that it might have been a genuine gesture...'

Olivia caught sight of his eyes glancing at the vase of roses in their lounge area.

'Don't even think about it, Jack! You know that I'd never do such a thing. I would give her the flowers directly, not leave them anonymously, for God's sake!'

'I know, I know – I didn't mean anything by it. But you know how fragile she is...' he retorted, holding up his hands defensively.

'We might be ex-wife and current wife, Jack, but we still have a reasonable relationship. You know that!'

Jack sighed. 'Anyway, it's now more than the rose thing. She thinks that someone is watching her from the garden in the dark. And then yesterday morning she found the wheelie-bin on its side with the lid open, and a few bits of paper strewn around. Some of her torn-up notes, and stuff. So now she thinks the prowler is going through her rubbish.'

'We live in the countryside, Jack. It's most likely a fox or stray cat looking for food.'

'That's what I told her. I also reminded her that it happened every now and again when we lived there.' He paused, and kept his eyes downcast. Talking about his past life with Alana always made him feel uncomfortable. 'But here's the weird thing – if it was a fox, then it's a damned clever fox...'

Olivia looked at Jack quizzically, not quite understanding his meaning.

'Whoever, or whatever it was, left a paper-trail down the front path and part way down the lane, vanishing off into the hedgerow. Alana noticed the bits of paper when she went out for her run, and recognised them as pieces of her edited manuscript.'

'Her manuscript…?' Olivia gave him a puzzled look.

'Yep. She has a deep distrust of the cloud system for saving documents, so prints off all her revised work at the end of each writing session, then tears up the edited pages. I can understand her nervousness – it's a lot of work to lose!'

'True,' concurred Olivia. 'I guess I would feel the same way if I had months of detailed work at risk.'

'So, she's asked me to fit a couple of those security cameras – one overlooking the bin and front door area, and one monitoring the back garden.'

'But I thought that there was plenty of external lighting to keep things secure? There are the coach-lights either side of the front door, then some spotlights at the back, if I remember rightly.'

'You do remember rightly, my love. I checked them, but they're not working. Probably rain in the electrics, or blown bulbs. Anyway, I'm going to ask an electrician to go and take a look at the lighting, and get a price from the alarm company to install a couple of security cameras.'

Olivia rolled her eyes. 'Jack – in case you've forgotten, she's there as an Airbnb guest for a month. Yes, I know she's your ex-wife, but this is a business arrangement. It might be Alana's old home, but it's now a holiday let. And let's face it, getting a solid booking for a full month is welcome money.' She laughed, trying to lighten the growing tension. 'After all, what tourist in their right mind would want to go hiking in the Peak District at the height of the midge season? Or the summer drizzle. Not many…'

Jack felt like he was torn between the devil and the deep blue sea. 'You're right. Not many,' he conceded. 'But she's here for four more weeks, until the end of the month. I'd rather do this little job and get her off my back, than listen to her nagging. Besides, it's a good security measure, and might even reduce the house insurance a bit.'

Not wanting to inflame the situation any further, Olivia nodded. 'But just this one job. It's a business we're running...'. She didn't need to finish her sentence. Jack understood her message, loud and clear, which made it all the more difficult for him to lead into the next thing.

'By the way...' He cleared his throat before quietly continuing, 'I invited her to come to the pub with us this evening...' Jack waited for a response, but was met with only silence. He cautiously looked up from his coffee. 'It's the pub-quiz, remember? First Sunday of the month. I thought it would be a bit of fun for the three of us; help take her mind off things. We could make a team.'

Olivia met his gaze, then smiled to mask her inner fury. 'Great! We might as well make a night of it, and eat out there, too. Best steak and ale pie in the area...'

Jack sensed that he'd crossed the "wives" line.

Just a little.

Chapter 9

More Questions Than Answers

Sunday 2nd August, 2015

The pub was already alive with convivial chatter, bursts of raucous laughter, and the chink of glasses when Alana, Jack and Olivia walked into The Wheatsheaf; the warm and cosy atmosphere a welcome retreat from the early August drizzle. Hungry patrons were already tucking into their pies, or fish, or mixed grill meals, the smell of which became a tempting lure for a rumbling, empty belly.

After shaking the drizzle off their coats and hanging them up, Alana went to find a table, while Jack and Olivia went to the bar to order drinks and food, having already made their choices from the *Tonight's Specials* chalk-board. The pub quiz was due to start at 8pm, so they would comfortably have time to eat, then register and pay to participate. Alana chose a table where she could meld into the background, much preferring to be a people-watcher than being the point of others' observations. She loved to watch the quirks, hand-gestures and facial expressions of folk, some of which invariably made its way into her writing. This naturalism helped to bring her characters to life and give them genuine, human dynamics. She often wondered if people could recognise themselves in her work.

She began systematically working her way along each table, casually smiling and nodding at people; waving the odd 'hi' to those she recognised, or those who recognised her. Who could be a likely candidate? There was a table full of elderly domino players; Alana grinned to herself – they were definite no-nos... They could hardly walk to the bar or toilets, let alone hang around in back gardens! A group of rowdy teens at the dart board never even looked her way when she came in and sat down – anyway, young folk had the reading stamina of a goldfish. If life wasn't controlled by an app, then they were not interested. It was highly unlikely that they'd read any of her novels. Simon from the butcher's shop caught her eye and gave her a little wave. A blush rose to his cheeks when she smiled and waved back. Maybe it was Simon? He would often slip in an extra pork chop, or a couple of sausages with a friendly wink when she used to shop there. Her author's mind slipped into fertile overdrive... What if it wasn't even a man? Maybe there was some woman in the village who was jealous of her success? Or maybe it was Olivia, as a way of warning her to keep away from Jack? No – that would be too obvious...

'Here you go, J20 Apple and Raspberry, no ice. I think I remembered your favourite tipple...' Jack placed her drink carefully onto the little table mat.

'Thanks. Yes, you remembered!' Her smile was one of a minor ex-wife victory; one that said, "See, he might now be married to you, but he hasn't forgotten the little details about me".

'The food will be about twenty minutes. Busy, isn't it?' Jack looked around at the quickly filling-up pub. He sat down opposite Alana, Olivia joining him by his side.

'By the way, I called an electrician today, Mick Herbert. Says he'll pop round in the morning to take a look at the lights. And I've spoken to the alarm company – they'll send an engineer a week on Monday. It's the soonest they can book us in.' Jack looked at Alana, and could see an immediate relaxation in her shoulders. She gave him a thumbs-up and nodded her thanks.

'Should be a good night for the pub quiz. Some tasty looking prizes for the top three teams.' He eyed up the baskets of goodies on the bar, all donated by local businesses; the usual offerings of a Chocolates & Wine combo, a Derbyshire Cheese hamper, and a gourmet Meat-Feast.

Alana toyed with her drink for a moment, before raising her glass. 'Well, cheers – and may the best team win... Which is us, of course!' She laughed at her own joke, a cover for the sudden wave of insecurity at being with her ex and his wife, while surrounded by a pub full of potential prowlers. That was the problem – there was no set profile for a prowler or stalker...

'It's really kind of you both to drop me back at the cottage.' Alana fumbled with the seat-belt, eager to get out.

Jack parked the Volvo onto the soft grass verge in front of the low stone wall. 'No problem. We wouldn't expect you to walk back in the dark.' He took note that all the lights were on inside, and sensed Alana's slowed reactions when stepping out of the car into the darkness. 'Tell you what, let me help you inside with the cheese basket, and just give things a quick check around. Great prize, by the way. And only fitting that you should have it, seeing as how the final question was about one of your books!'

Alana laughed. 'Hmm, but that got us a few shouts of "fix" from the locals... But then again, I love Hartington cheeses, so I'm not going to argue with getting second prize. Are you sure that you guys don't want any?'

'No, you enjoy them. We're trying to cut back on our dairy intake at the moment,' said Olivia. 'Jack's cholesterol is a little on the high side.'

Jack jokingly scowled his disapproval towards Olivia, mimicking her comments, 'Jack's cholesterol is a little on the high side, meh, meh, meh. Let's deny him some cheese, meh, meh, meh...', before hopping out and coming around to help Alana. He reached onto the back seat for the cheese basket, and gave it a "goodbye" hug, in order to tease his wife. He blew her a kiss. 'I won't be a moment, love. I'm just going to take Alana in, and make sure that everything is secure for her.'

Olivia gave a poker-face smile, masking the cauldron bubbling away under her surface. 'No problem, take your time.'

Only four more weeks, then Alana would be gone...

Chapter 10

Floral Tribute

Monday 3rd August, 2015

The flagstone patio area was filled with the heady fragrance from the old rambling rose, as the mid-morning sun warmed their blooms and released their scent. Bumble bees lazily droned from flower to flower, loading their little leg baskets with precious cargoes of golden pollen. Alana inhaled deeply and tilted her face towards the sun. She closed her eyes to shield them from the intense brightness. It had been days since the weather had been decent enough to sit outdoors, and she welcomed the opportunity to take a fresh-air break with her morning coffee. The flow of editing and revising was going well, having now found a working rhythm to her retreat environment.

Peak FM hummed away on the radio in the background, keeping the deep, internal silence of the cottage at bay, while countryside sounds contributed to the outside symphony: a combined harvester droning away in the field beyond, a pair of crows wheeling and fighting, flying high and low as they circled each other, claws tangled together, their cawing sounds shrill. A gentle breeze rustled the leaves of the shrubbery and trees; a palette of greens and summer colours – no longer the foreboding dark tones of the night. Droplets of overnight dew sparkled like scattered diamonds on the grass, as the sun moved around the garden.

Yet an almost overwhelming sense of heaviness pulled down on her psyche. Her surroundings, her success, her general good health, all pointed towards a "life is good" scenario. But there was something that clung to her back like a dead weight; like an invisible Siamese twin. She recalled the countless times when she had had to draw heavily on her mantra of "tomorrow will be a better day", just to stop herself from spiralling into another depression; that was a dark place which she had no desire to revisit. She knew that she had much to be grateful for.

Alana checked her watch – 11:20. Didn't Jack say that the electrician would be stopping by at 11:30 to come and take a look at the external lighting? He should be here any minute…

Her mind unconsciously drifted towards Jack. Funny how things work out… Jack had literally saved her arse from the first moment, when she had slipped on some black ice in front of his office just as he was coming out of the door to go to lunch. He had been the chivalrous knight in shining armour, insisting that he got her to the hospital, and stayed with her while her arm was X-rayed. Obviously he had wanted to keep a check on the damsel that he had rescued… The rest, as they say, is history. For the fifteen years that they had been together and married, he had nursed her through dark depressions and a breakdown. Alana had decided that she really hadn't been a great catch after all and pushed him away. He deserved better. Although reluctant at first, Jack knew that it was a lost cause, and succumbed to her request for a divorce. Alana wafted a bee away from her head, and checked her watch again. She absently tapped the watch-face with her index finger. Anyway, Jack seemed happy now – he had Olivia, and she, being ten years his junior, was keeping him on his toes. Having met her on a joint renovation project, he'd moved away from the cosy cottage lifestyle into her grand, open-plan barn conversion. And in keeping with Olivia's profession as an interior designer, Jack had even once joked that their life was literally "fifty shades of white, with a few bold-statement scatter cushions".

Alana's reverie was interrupted by the clatter of the brass door knocker.

At last! She carefully put her coffee mug onto the little outdoor table and went through to the front entrance.

As Alana opened the front door, she was stunned to be met with a bouquet of flowers and a smiling florist, rather than the electrician.

'Ms McQueen?'

'Erm... Y-yes... That's me.'

'Here's a delivery for you. Beautiful, aren't they? I love white roses, particularly when they're mixed with Baby's Breath. Such a peaceful looking arrangement.'

Misreading Alana's puzzled face as one of anger, the florist stammered an apology. 'I'm sorry about the gift tag – it dropped out of the bouquet as I was coming up the path and fell in a puddle. It's a little bit dirty. Sorry... I think you can still read the message.'

Alana could feel her pulse starting to race. 'N...No, no, it's okay, really. Thanks...' She turned to close the door, and gave a weak smile to the florist. 'Thanks...'

Puzzled, Alana took the bouquet into the kitchen. She had no idea if there were any vases now that the cottage was run as Airbnb accommodation, so set the flowers in the sink while she fumbled for the gift card.

"Thank you for still caring. W..." in typed, printed letters.

Dirty water from the puddle had smudged the sender's name. She tried to take a closer look, but could only make out the first letter – W. Were the other letters part of a name, or initials? It was hard to tell. It looked like three letters. What name began with W, and was three letters long? None that she could think of. She looked on the other side of the gift card – *Stemz Florist*. Perhaps if she gave them a call?

But that would have to wait until later, the electrician having just arrived. It was turning into one of those days...

From his top-field position, nestled among the golden wheat stalks, he focused the binoculars towards the cottage. Daytime meant that he had to be further away, thereby lessening the risk of being seen. And as the fields were now one-by-one being harvested, there were fewer and fewer secluded vantage points from which he could observe. Activity by the gate caught his attention. What was that? A little van? Who could it be? He lay down, stock-still. His vision followed the florist as she went up the path, then knocked on the front door. Great! This would be an opportunity to see Alana. But who was sending her flowers? A bouquet of flowers, no less! A burst of inadequacy flooded through him, warming his cheeks. All he could do was steal a rose to give her – and a rose from her old garden, at that.

Well, if someone was sending her flowers, then he would just have to top that, wouldn't he! As he formulated a gift-plan, his binocular-vision caught sight of someone else walking up the path. Busy today at Woodend Cottage! He was less pleased to see that this visitor was a man, albeit one carrying a tool-kit. Obviously an innocent visitor – lovers don't usually come with tool-kits.

Curiosity chewed into him. Time to change position, and take a long-shot look from the fields at the back.

***

'What do you mean, you can't tell me who sent the flowers? Don't you have a name?' Alana tapped her pen on the notepad, agitated.

'I'm sorry, Ms McQueen, but with the privacy laws and everything, I can't give you any personal details as to who paid for the flowers. I can only tell you the name that was on the gift card.'

'That's ridiculous! No-one knows where I'm staying at the moment! How would anyone know where to send flowers to? Did you give out any of *my* personal information?' In her shocked fury, Alana had completely overlooked the fact that she had been out and about in the village, that she'd been to the pub with Jack and Olivia, and had also posted on social media that she was staying at a countryside retreat in the Peak while working on her current writing project.

The florist sighed at the other end of the phone. 'All I can say is that the order was received yesterday evening via our website order form, to be delivered today, Monday. And that the card was to read "Thank you for still caring. WRS".'

'But I don't know anyone with the initials WRS!' Alana looked at the phone as if it would change the information, before returning it to her ear. 'Okay, okay. Thanks, anyway...' She disconnected the call, and threw her phone down onto the countertop, perturbed that she was still none the wiser.

She looked at the bouquet and felt a tsunami of nervous adrenaline flood her system.

Just who the hell is WRS? And how does WRS know where to send the flowers?

Driven by agitation and fury, Alana snatched the bouquet out of the sink, and marched it out to the dustbin, almost knocking the electrician off his ladder as he repaired the outdoor lighting.

'Are you okay, missus?'

'What?'

'Are you okay, missus? You look like you've seen a ghost, or had a shock...'

Alana closed her eyes and took a few deep nasal breaths. 'I'm sorry... Yes, yes, I'm fine. Sorry if I almost knocked you over. It's just...' She shook her head, trying to find words that wouldn't come. 'I'm fine.'

Mind's Eye

I am eleven...

"*Although I never really settled into school life at the Infants School in Castle Ridge, being at Junior School wasn't so bad. It was a small, old fashioned red-brick school building with high, arched windows, located right next door to Castle Ridge Castle. Just that in-itself made the school feel special.*

The transition from infants to juniors brought a little more maturity among us kids, and I somehow managed to make it onto the fringes of friendship groups – I tried so hard to be one of them. The early Eighties were upon us, and we were being influenced by all the new boy bands such as Duran Duran, Spandau Ballet, Wham! and Culture Club. And watching Top of the Pops, of course – we all wanted to be dancers like Legs & Co. If it was trendy or had a cute smile and haircut, we loved it!

I seemed to be a natural with reading and writing – my "reading-age" was way above average according to the tests, and I loved writing stories and poems. I suppose this was my escape world. As for maths, well... I could manage the basics – I preferred letters to numbers. And so came the 11-Plus exams – the ones which would determine which senior school we would go to. For us, the choice was either Castle Ridge Comprehensive, or (if you passed the 11-Plus), Shirecliffe Grammar.

Most of the kids in my year were destined for the local comp. I passed the 11-Plus, so was en-route to the grammar school. There has always been a terrible rivalry between these two schools, and kids from Castle Ridge who ended up going to the grammar school usually got bullied or beaten up. At least, that was the rumour.

Luckily, I managed to persuade my parents to get me a transfer to the local comprehensive school, so I could at least be among the kids that I knew. What I hadn't realised, was that kids from other junior schools in the area would also converge here. And these were kids with an estate-reputation...

The concept of the school uniform was, and still is, to equalise the students – this is all well and good if your uniform fits, or is clean. Nor if you have to use a hand-me-down leather satchel, when all the other kids have got cool school bags. And God help you if you have spots or limp, greasy hair.

I had all of the above.

So that became the start of my high school nightmares – I was no better off at the comp than I would have been at the neighbouring grammar school. Taunts and teasing became my daily bread – sniggering behind my back, just loud enough for me to hear. They were lonely years.

As if home-life wasn't bad enough, school life once again became Hell..."

Chapter 11

(Anti)social Media

Tuesday 4th August, 2015

B efore starting her day of editing, Alana logged into her social media accounts to check the news and updates, and add a few cursory likes and comments. It was always good to keep one's name in the media spotlight, even if only at a low-key level. Never post anything controversial, and only write comments that are complimentary not contradictory. Basically, if you can't say anything nice, then it was better to say nothing at all. That was Alana's non-negotiable golden rule.

Facebook was full of the usual blah, blah, blah of people either having a nice life, or screaming about some injustice somewhere in the world. She checked the updates for her author-page, and felt her ego inflate a little with a clutch of "likes" to her cheese-hamper picture and "thank-you" post about the fun that she'd had on Sunday night at the pub-quiz. Always good to acknowledge the positives in the community. She had also gained five new followers, most of which she recognised as locals, except for one, who appeared to be a fellow writer under the guise of *Shakespeare's Apprentice* (no real name given). The profile picture was of Shakespeare's Globe theatre, and the background picture was made up of a collage of different works by writers all called William: *Tyger Tyger* by Blake, *Lord of the Flies* by Golding, and *Romeo & Juliet*, by Shakespeare himself. Clearly this person liked anything by writers called William! A little obsessive, maybe? Alana recalled her own schooldays, having studied *Lord of the Flies*. My goodness, what a grim story that was! A cursory scan of recent posts by *Shakespeare's Apprentice* revealed nothing more sinister than poetry, literary quotes and humorous memes. She decided not to dig any further into this account, grateful for this new batch of followers.

A quick visit to her Instagram account showed that she had had a clutch of new likes to her most recent post. Although Alana only posted updates every few days, she could fully understand the addiction of getting likes. It wasn't often that she received negative comments (which, she conceded, stung like a knife), but when she did, she would calm her disappointment by using the mantra that people were entitled to air their point of view, so left it at that. Never engage in an exchange of differing opinions. It just wasn't worth the negativity. A handful of new people had also started following her, which led her down the rabbit hole of checking them out. Being cautious by nature, Alana had taken to vetting the profiles of her new IG followers, removing any that she considered too creepy, or autobots. Why did people hide behind these strange names and identities instead of just being themselves? Another thing that annoyed her was the fact that some accounts were private, so it was impossible to judge what kind of person they were by looking at their posts. She noticed one of her new followers was one of these hidden private-account people – *WRS_85*. Even the profile picture didn't show anything about this person – it was just a feather quill pen in an inkpot!

...*WRS_85*...

...*WRS*...

Ho-ly fuck!

Alana felt the bile rise from her stomach and sting the back of her throat...

They were the same initials as the gift tag on the flowers!

Surely it must be a coincidence?

Surely...?

She quickly threw her phone onto the table as though it was covered in something disgusting, narrowly missing her cup of tea. Frozen moments passed while her composure returned. She rubbed her face and massaged her temples; the pulse of her heartbeat clearly felt. It had to be one and the same person.

Is it someone from my past? Eighty-five...could that be a year, perhaps? Maybe a birth-year? WRS_85 – who do I know that was born in 1985? That was thirty years ago...

Alana racked the dark recesses of her brain.

I was born in 1973. So it's unlikely to be anyone from school... I would have been twelve in 1985. Who did I know back then?

Her mind hopscotched through her circle of friends (such as it was) at the time, but no-one came to mind with those initials. She reached for her phone and slid it across the table towards her, the screen face down. Cautiously, she flipped it over and logged back in. The anonymous profile of *WRS_85* stared at her again. Although Alana felt compelled to remove this new follower, some inner voice told her to leave it for the time being...

More detective work would be needed before she "closed the case" on this one.

Chapter 12

Nine Lives

Wednesday 5th August, 2015

'Here puss, puss, puss...'

The ginger moggy skulked across the top of the hay bales, ready to pounce on the dead mouse that he was teasing it with. Even though she was a feral "old ratting-cat", as he'd once heard the farmer call her, they'd developed quite a bond of trust over the years that he'd been using the barn as his night bed. She'd even let him cuddle some of the kittens that she'd produced.

Her claws dug into the soft, not-yet-stiff body of the mouse, before flipping it into the air. She pounced again, then bit into it. She had won her prize for entertaining him for a few minutes. The feral cats that lived around the barns and outbuildings were usually enough to keep the rats and mice at manageable levels, but now that the barns were filling with the fresh hay bales, the farmer had increased his protection by adding traps loaded with poisoned bait. Sadly, this had also taken the lives of one or two cats after they had stolen mice from the traps, much to the annoyance of the farmer.

Rays from the setting sun filtered through the slats in the barn wall, enhancing the golden glow of the hay and ginger cat. A golden world soon to be captured and taken over by the twilight. He watched the cat as she first washed her paws, then washed her ears and face. Like him, she was scraggy and scrawny, begging scraps of food wherever she could find them. But she was proud, sitting there like Queen Bee – the queen of the farmyard. She was probably the oldest cat here. And so he decided to name her Queenie.

And Queenie would become the gift to his princess.

Chapter 13

A Doorstep Gift

Thursday 6th August, 2015

'What do you mean, "There's a dead cat on the patio"? – A note? – No, I can't come over right now, I'm just about to go into a meeting. What does it say on the note? – Are you sure?' Jack held the phone away from his ear and looked at it, his brow furrowed in disbelief. He could still hear Alana's ranting voice, even from this distance. 'Look, just take a photo of it. – Yes, as evidence. Then put a towel over it, or something. – No, I'll stop by on my way home from work. – Yes, I promise.'

Jack's stomach rolled over as he mulled on the conversation that he'd just had with his very distressed ex-wife – a distress that was justified, having just returned from her morning jog to find a dead cat on the back patio.

A dead cat with a dirty, hand-printed note tied with baling twine around its neck, "From Your No. 1 Fan xx".

Having read all of her books, Jack surmised that whoever had done this could be familiar with Alana's work. There was a dead cat left on someone's doorstep in *Scab!*, one of her novels – albeit without the note. That was an added extra, in this case. Leaving a rose was one thing, but this was taking fandom to the next level. Random, sick and bizarre. He quickly sent a message to Olivia to let her know that he would be late home this evening as he needed to stop by at the cottage, only to receive an angry-face emoji as a reply. Jack rubbed his chin while he thought out his reply-message. His only option was to describe what Alana had found, and hoped that Olivia would now understand... This time he received a green-faced puking emoji.

She understood.

Alana disconnected the call and continued to pace back and forth in the kitchen, chewing on her bottom lip. She could feel a nauseous wave of adrenaline pumping around her body, causing her hands to tremble.

Why? Why would somebody do this? What did they have to gain?

Feeling faint, she sat down at the kitchen table and tried to regulate her breathing. Jack had told her to put a towel over the cat, but first she would need to take a photo "as evidence". Did he mean it would have to be reported as a crime? The cat didn't look like it was wearing a collar when she took a cursory look. In fact, it looked positively mangy and flea-ridden; like one of the feral strays from the farm nearby. Why would she have to report it? Surely no-one would miss an old farm cat? Maybe it was the farmer who had done it – a sick kind of homage to her writing? You never know with people these days... She geared herself for the task ahead.

Red-pink foam oozed from the mouth of the deceased feline, and formed a watery pool around its head. Alana watched, repulsed yet fascinated. The cat's face was contorted into a death mask, with bulging eyes and tongue; testimony to its agonising final moments. It was safe to assume that the cat hadn't died of natural causes. She gently poked the corpse with a piece of old garden cane, and used it to lever the note from around the cat's neck. There was something about the handwriting that looked similar to the writing on the tag with the red rose. Could it be the same person? If only she hadn't thrown them away. But then again, she hadn't expected to receive something like this...

Alana noticed that the cat's body was already beginning to stiffen slightly with rigor mortis, so it must have been dead for a couple of hours, at least. It somehow didn't feel right to take a photograph of the poor old moggie; surely it should be left to rest in peace after its tortures? It felt like an invasion of the soul's privacy. But then again, police did it all the time at crime scenes. Reluctantly, she withdrew her phone from her hoodie pocket and took a few photos: one full body, and then some close-ups of the face and the note.

'Sorry, kitty...'. Though her stomach lurched at the grim scene, she found herself becoming conversely intrigued as she zoomed in on the reality of death. The contorted face. The pink froth and blood. The bloated tongue. The bulging eyes...

At least the alarm company would be coming after the weekend to install the security system. Hopefully whoever was doing all these things would be caught on camera. A worrying thought passed through Alana's mind – both she and Jack would have a phone-app to monitor the cameras. That meant Jack would be able to watch her every move at the cottage. Or even worse, the security company could monitor her if they wanted. A surge of nervous energy caused her stomach to flutter – she would never know if or when she was being observed, or by whom... Could this feeling of constantly being watched get any worse!

Maybe this was the cat that had left the dead mouse (she had almost stepped on it!) and the dead robin on the front doorstep recently. After all, that's what cats do – they bring little "gifts" and leave them for their owner. Not that she was the owner of this cat, but maybe that's what it had decided. The cat might have thought it an ideal gift, but Alana had been shocked to the core. She swore that if she ever got her hands on the cat that had done it... A sentiment she now regretted.

She stroked the body and shuddered. At least it had eaten some of the cat food and milk mixture that she'd put out for the hedgehogs

– the dish was almost empty. It had had a final meal before dying. As she looked closer, she noticed some strange greenish-brown lumps mixed in with the cat food. Her brow furrowed – this was definitely not something that she'd put in with the food. A cold feeling ran over her skin, causing goosebumps and the hairs on her forearms to stand on end. Someone had been *THAT* close to the house...

A jumble of thoughts zoomed around her mind. It was probably safe to assume that whatever was in the cat food was poisonous – perhaps it would be best to get rid of the corpse so that it wouldn't come into contact with other creatures? Yes, that's what she needed to do! Maybe it was only right to give the cat a decent burial, feral or not. She really didn't want to leave it on the patio all day until Jack stopped by after work. It no longer seemed appropriate. A coffin... She needed to make a coffin. Maybe there was a large cornflake box in the kitchen? Or a shoe box somewhere?

As Alana stood up to go inside, her eyes caught sight of something by the plant-pots on the edge of the patio. Piqued by curiosity, she went to investigate. It was an old, rolled up sack-cloth bag, like the type used for bagging potatoes. She picked it up and gave it a shake. Alana screamed and jumped back as the stiff corpses of two dead mice fell onto the ground, together with a handful of greenish-brown pellets. Rat-poison, maybe?

Who on earth could do such a thing?

Realising that this was probably connected to the "cat crime", she returned the sack-cloth to the exact spot where she had found it, before taking a photo. Alana pondered the scene for a moment. Would she also need to keep the bag and mice as possible evidence? Probably not – it was unlikely to contain any viable fingerprints. Another thought struck her – perhaps burying a poisoned moggie wasn't a particularly environmentally-friendly option. What if someone were to inadvertently dig it up while gardening? How long did the residues of poison last? She didn't want to be responsible for something like that.

Geared on by the need to safely dispose of the poisonous remains, Alana went into the kitchen to find some rubber gloves and a rubbish bag, before cautiously gathering up the sack-cloth, food dish and animal corpses.

Satisfied that the scene was clean and poison-free, she unceremoniously dumped the black bag into the wheelie-bin and slammed the lid closed in defiance.

Alana shivered and looked around. As an afterthought, she peeled off the gloves and threw those into the bin alongside the package of death, before sticking up two fingers to whoever might be watching...

And she was being watched.

From his safe vantage point, he focused the binoculars on her face. Somehow, Alana didn't look very happy at finding Queenie...

He hadn't meant to hurt the darned cat – he had wanted to leave her as a live gift. But she had scratched, and spit, and bit him as he tried to put her in the cloth bag. She had left him no choice. She had to be subdued...

The more he watched Alana, the more he became hurt and confused. He had only wanted to make her happy. To give her something nice. Why would she throw his humble gift into the bin? It wasn't like he had the money to give her anything fancy. He swallowed hard, his pride dented.

Ungrateful bitch!

* * *

'So, what's the update on the cat-thing?' Olivia busied herself laying the table ready for dinner, while Jack selected a bottle of wine. 'Not that I want to think about it, just before we eat... How awful for Alana.'

Jack shook his head. 'After all that huffing and puffing, and harassing me at work, she had thrown everything away by the time I got there. For some reason, she thought the cat had been poisoned, and didn't want to leave something like that lying around. Then she decided that she didn't want the police involved, and deleted the photos.'

'I'm beginning to think that she made it all up. There never really was any dead cat.' Olivia directly looked at Jack. 'I think it was just some fantasy – some ploy – to have you on a string.'

'C'mon, Liv, that's a bit unfair...' countered Jack.

'Unfair? Not really. I mean, think about it – she's a writer. It's her job to make fiction sound convincing – to sound like fact. That's how readers get drawn into a book, because it's been written with such realism, even when it's fiction. Did you even take a look in the dustbin?'

'No... But then again, the dustbin collection was today. The bin had been emptied by the time I got there.'

Olivia raised her eyebrows and cocked her head. 'See what I mean. A suitably believable but gruesome story, conveniently told on dustbin-day. And you fell for it...'

Jack looked at Olivia, his eyes wide, mouth open. 'I can't believe you just said that! That you would accuse Alana of something so, so...' He huffed while he thought of a way to describe his disbelief at Olivia's snide judgement. 'There's no way that Alana could have known it was the bin-collection today. *You* never remember the day, and you live here! How would she know? Of course she wasn't using this as a convenient excuse to get me to come over. Who in their right mind would dream up such a scenario!'

'Okay, fine! Side with Alana if you have to,' she retorted. 'But I don't believe it for a minute. You mark my words, she's got you on a string.'

Sensing that they were at a stalemate, Jack refrained from taking the argument any further. They had both made up their minds on what they considered to be the truth of the situation. He believed Alana – there was no reason for her to make up such a gruesome story.

Was there?

He uncorked the bottle of red, and poured himself a generous glass.

Chapter 14

Airing Clean Laundry

Friday 7th August, 2015

Grateful for the fine weather, Alana used the opportunity to catch up with some much-needed laundry, having only brought two weeks' worth of clothes. She neatly pegged the freshly laundered clothing onto the rotary dryer, ensuring that everything was equally spaced and accordingly grouped into jeans, tee-shirts, hoodies, underwear and socks. Alana took a deep breath, uncomfortable at seeing her knickers and bras on the line – lingerie made such a statement about one's personality. And it was clear for the world to see that Alana's had to be matching. In fact, it was clear for the world to see that the colour of her underwear *and* socks matched the colour of her tee-shirts. To Alana, it was one of those "what if I have an accident?" types of neuroses – she couldn't bear the thought of being taken to casualty in dirty, mismatched clothing.

She headed back inside, gently swinging the wicker laundry basket by the handle as she strolled across the garden. That was the beauty of a long-term stay in a house or cottage – this kind of rental usually had a washing machine, so one only needed to take a limited amount of clothing. The downside was (a) trying to figure out how to use the washing machine, and (b) actually making the effort to do the laundry! Plus you were at the mercy of using the owner's choice of wash-powder and fabric softener. Luckily for Alana, the choice of Olivia's laundry products was reasonable quality. But unluckily for her, she'd just used the last of each, so felt obliged to replace them. A trip into Buxton was needed.

She grabbed her purse and shopping bag, and headed out.

The warmth of the late morning sunshine seeped through his overcoat. It was good to get some heat into the bones after walking in the cool shade of the woodland to freshen up. His feet felt damp, the moisture from the low growing vegetation having permeated through the leather of his old hiking boots. Freedom was good, but it came at a hand-me-down price. He settled himself into his usual vantage point, then took off his boots and socks to get some air to his feet, and dry them out. When you relied on walking everywhere, healthy feet were so important. He adjusted the binoculars towards the back garden of the cottage, pleased to see that there was already some activity; Alana was busy pegging some laundry onto the dryer. My, how careful she was! So neat! What a luxury to have all those clean clothes... A wry smile crossed his lips as he focused on the underwear. Typical Alana – all pretty and matching. He then followed her around the garden as she checked the flowers, and dead-headed a few of them. Alana then headed for the raspberry canes in the top corner of the garden and helped herself to a bowlful of ripe berries. Maybe he could sneak down there this evening and help himself to a handful... It had been ages since he'd had any. He frowned as she headed towards the French doors, drinking in every last step of her movements. The garden show seemed to be over for the time being. Perhaps she would come out again soon, with the weather being so nice? He tried to refocus so that he could see inside. Strange – she appeared to be locking the French doors. That could only mean one thing – Alana was going out. He quickly grabbed his socks and boots and moved further along the perimeter of the field so that he could adjust his position, and get a better view of the front door. His expectation was rewarded as she exited, little shopping bag in hand, and headed off down the lane.

Great! That would give him time to slip into the garden and grab what he needed...

***

Sainsbury's Local was already humming and buzzing with shoppers preparing for the weekend-shop. Conscious of the fact that she would have to walk back to the cottage with her bags of shopping, Alana just took a wire basket in order to keep the load manageable, particularly as she would have the added weight of wash-powder and softener as well as food. Experience had taught her not to use a trolley, and risk buying more than she could carry.

After trawling the chiller cabinets for some tasty inspiration, she settled on some salmon fillets dressed with a lime and mango sauce. A side dish of new potatoes, mixed salad and a fresh French baguette completed her menu. Summer was one of the best times for food! She gently squeezed some peaches to check their ripeness before selecting a couple. They would make a tasty addition to the fresh cottage raspberries and chopped mint leaves for dessert.

'Alana! Is that you? It is!'

A mop of curly red hair, framing the rosy cheeks and freckled face of Mrs Bullock from Woodend Farm, the farm near the cottage, appeared beside her, breaking her culinary train of thought. If ever there was a "typical farmer's wife", Mrs Bullock was it, complete with an apt surname. It was something which had amused Jack and Alana from the day they'd bought the cottage. At least Mrs B had refrained from going shopping in her wellies today...

'Jim said that he'd seen you the other day. Saw you taking a run down the lane. I've been meaning to pop over and say hello. Been meaning to bring you some eggs – the hens are laying like crazy at the moment. Must be the good weather. Anyway, how are you, dear? Haven't seen you in ages.'

Alana blinked a few times while she tried to process Mrs Bullock's mile-a-minute verbal exposé.

'I'm fine, thanks. Lovely to see you, Mrs B. Yes, I'm back at the cottage, but only until the 28th. I leave just before the Bank Holiday weekend. Trying to catch up with some writing, so thought I'd come out to the countryside.'

'Well, it's lovely to see you too, my dear. That's been the downside since you moved away. After your ex and his new missus turned the cottage into one of those holiday lets, we never know from one weekend to the next who our neighbours are going to be. Mostly townies who think they can traipse all over the land, or through the woods. Tch! I don't blame you for getting away before the Bank Holiday madness, that's for sure!'

Alana noticed that Mrs B already had a full trolley, making her own grocery selection look pitiful. She quickly plonked a hand of bananas and a punnet of strawberries into her own basket to make it look more appealing.

Mrs Bullock nodded towards the trolley. 'Well, that's me done. I'm going back your way, Alana – would you like a ride back to the cottage? It's no bother to drop you off...' Mrs B's smile was broad and genuine.

Alana could feel her chest tighten, stifling her breathing; a defensive auto-response to being offered a car ride. She began to fumble with her words. 'Erm, no, it's okay. I've only got this little lot, it's not heavy.' She waved her hand dismissively over the basket of shopping. 'Besides, the weather is so nice. I don't mind walking back.'

Her excuses were just met with a light laugh from the farmer's wife. 'Really? Oh, come on – I haven't seen you in ages. Are you really going to deny me a chance of some girly chit-chat?!'

Knowing that it would be virtually impossible to fend off the playful pushiness of Mrs Bullock, Alana swallowed down her nervousness and conceded defeat. 'Well, okay then. I've just got to pick up some milk, and then I'm done. Should I meet you out in the car park?'

Mrs B gave Alana the thumbs-up as she headed towards the checkout. 'I've still got the same old blue Defender. It's parked near one of the trolley bays.'

Oh, gawd! Not the stinky old Land Rover! Alana recalled the few occasions in the past when she'd reluctantly accepted a ride from the kindly farmer's wife; the interior positively hummed with farmyard smells...

***

'So, you're just finishing your next book, are you? I can't wait to read it. We've got all of your novels, you know! It's nice to read a book and know the person who wrote it.' Mrs Bullock absently chatted on, while Alana surreptitiously focused on trying to regulate her breathing. She had hoped to avoid sitting in the front, but the back seat was covered in rubbish and shopping, leaving her no choice. At least if she was breathing through her mouth, she would be lessening the rank smell of the Land Rover's interior. It was no better than when she last remembered it. Pungent and earthy. Alana wound down the window in order to let in some fresh air and help combat some of the dizziness.

Mrs Bullock laughed. 'Sorry, it's a bit smelly in here, isn't it!'

Alana wrinkled her nose playfully and nodded. She picked up the thread of Mrs B's book conversation. 'Thanks, that's nice to hear. I'll have to send you a signed copy once it's published. How does that sound?'

'Oooh, that would be nice! A book signed by the author.' Mrs B grinned, her face a picture of satisfaction. Her mind abruptly jumped to the next topic. 'Oh, yes, I almost forgot to tell you – that tramp is back again. Remember the one? He tends to stay in our old hay barn.

He's no trouble, keeps out of our way. Anyway, I just wanted to tell you, in case you saw him tramping around the fields, or whatever it is that tramps do all day.'

Alana's eyes widened. 'A tramp? I didn't know there was one around this area. I've never seen one.'

'Aye, he's lived on and off in these parts for years. He vanished for a while, not long after you left, so I assumed that he'd either tramped off somewhere else, or died. Then he came back again a few years ago. Been here ever since. But, like I say, he's no bother. Never done anyone any harm. Just wanted to give you the heads up in case you caught sight of him wandering about the lanes or fields.'

'Thanks, Mrs B. I'll keep that in mind.'

'Well, here we are. That didn't take long.' She pulled up onto the grass verge in front of the cottage so that Alana could get out.

'Thanks for the ride home. Have a nice weekend...' Alana grabbed her shopping bag from the back seat and readied herself to climb out of the Land Rover.

'You too, my dear. In fact, why don't you come over on Sunday afternoon? We were thinking of having a barbecue if the weather is nice.'

The invitation caught Alana off-guard. 'Erm... Yes, sure. Thanks, that sounds great. What time should I come over?'

'Come over for around five-ish. And before you ask, you don't need to bring anything, and yes, it's okay to wear jeans!'

Alana laughed. 'Well, that's answered all my unasked questions! See you Sunday afternoon, then.'

'Look forward to it, my dear. And I know that Jim will be happy to see you again. He'll be in seventh heaven having a famous author come to tea!'

'Well, I would hardly call myself famous, but, thanks...'

As she made her way up the front garden path, her eyes couldn't help but dart from side to side. Her stomach fluttered with unease.

So, there's an old tramp living nearby... Surely it couldn't be him responsible for all these happenings? No, Mrs B said that he doesn't cause any trouble...

Yet when she discovered that her laundry had been tampered with on the rotary dryer, and a set of underwear had gone missing, Alana couldn't help but feel that Mrs B might just be wrong.

Those security cameras would be not only welcome, but essential, if she was to survive to the end of the month.

Chapter 15

A Day in the Life of...

Friday 7th August, 2015

"So, how did I get to this point? How did I become a free-walker? I much prefer thinking of myself as a free-walker, and not a tramp.

Let's start at the beginning –

Like Elaine, I was an only-child. But unlike Elaine, I was loved and cherished. We might not have been a wealthy family, but we managed. Sadly, that all changed after my dad collapsed and died at a fairly young age. He didn't have any life insurance – he didn't believe in anything like that. So, that left me and Mum struggling along until the money ran out. She could no longer afford to pay the mortgage, so we joined the merry band of council-house tenants down on the estate in Castle Ridge. The estate was a blend of council houses and NCB houses. Rough, but it was home.

I followed my dream of becoming a car mechanic, starting an apprenticeship at a local dealership, and day-release to Chesterfield College. I even managed to save enough money to buy my dream car – an XR3i.

And lucky me – as well as my dream car, I got my dream girl – Elaine McCairn. She'd had a rough life as a young 'un, but managed to dig her way out of poverty once she got a few pocket-money jobs. I admired that quality in her – she knew that she was worth so much more than the shit-show she'd been born into.

But we all know how dreams can very easily turn into nightmares...

You know about the accident that we were involved in? The one that cruelly claimed the life of that little boy. Life was never the same after that. I couldn't face driving a car, which meant that I lost my job. After all, what garage wants a mechanic that refuses to drive? Things became crazy – we both buried our shock, grief and fear in booze and wild living, at least for a while. Then the fights and arguments started. Elaine no longer wanted to live like that – she'd already had her fair share of being caught up in the alcoholic lifestyle via her parents. It wasn't for her. The gossip machine and accusations continued to grind us down, so Elaine decided that enough was enough. She left Castle Ridge, and walked out of my life.

Me? I hit the bottle with a vengeance.

And as if things weren't already bad enough, I lost my mum to cancer, and lost the council house because I didn't prioritise paying the rent.

I became a homeless drunk, with nothing to my name but a carrier bag full of clothes. I managed to find casual work here and there, paid in cash. But, of course, the cash went straight into the tills of the nearest boozer. It didn't help my work prospects by turning up still half pissed, so work eventually dried up. Life became a series of begging, sleeping rough, and stealing what I could to survive. You know that you've reached rock bottom when you find yourself skulking around the back of pub yards, drinking dregs from the empties and eating left-over food from the bins...

I confess to feeling jealous of Elaine's success when I stumbled across her book-promotion poster. I knew it was her, even with the name change. Alana McQueen – where did she dig that name up from! A posh twist on Elaine McCairn, I suppose. And so I began to follow her around – to follow my lost love. I found out where she lived, and that she had a man about the house. It only served to fuel my jealousy and resentment...

Then came a breakthrough – it appeared that she and the man split up! Although I knew that I would never be in with a chance to get back with her, I still followed her to Manchester when she moved away. That was a big mistake. The city is the worst place for a free-walker. They treat you like shit on their shoes. It wasn't safe. I didn't deserve to be spat on. I didn't deserve to be beaten up.

So I conceded my defeat, and headed back to the countryside. I remembered that the farm near Elaine's old cottage had a few barns dotted around, so that's where I made my "home". The farmer soon figured out that someone was sleeping rough in the old hay barn. I remember him coming in one night while I was hunkered down, out of sight. He simply said, "I know you're in here. All that I ask is that you don't steal from me, and don't set any fires. And keep out of my sight." I've pretty much managed to keep to that. I'm grateful to have somewhere warm and dry for the night, and for the winter. The farmer's wife sometimes leaves a pint of milk, or some pie for me. I can always guess which day is Sunday – that's when she leaves me a bit of roast beef, or some cheese and pork pie. Bless her, she left me this old overcoat, too.

Even the good people of Buxton have become accustomed to me. A lady from one of the charity shops once came outside to give me a woolly jumper, and some "new" boots. And if I time it just right, the bakery will sometimes give me a few of the day's leftovers. There are some kind, compassionate people in this world.

Booze? No, I don't drink any more. Can't afford it. Besides, it did my life and health no good. Good riddance to it.

And now I have the good fortune to have Elaine back in my life – kind of.

But will she see it that way?"

Chapter 16

William

Saturday 8th August, 2015

Alana's focused concentration was broken by the *ping* of her phone. She stared at it, then back at her computer screen, torn between the two.

Damn!

Knowing that it would be a lost cause, she grabbed up her phone with the intention of putting it on silent.

Well, maybe just check this notification, then put it on silent...

Her eyes widened with curiosity when she saw who the message had come from.

"Shakespeare's Apprentice would like to send you a message. Opening the message means that you will be connected on Messenger."

She shrugged to herself, then opened the message from a fellow writer.

"Sorry to trouble you, Ms McQueen, but I just wondered if the flowers had arrived safely? They should have been delivered to you on Monday."

Alana blinked, stunned, while she considered her next move. Her instinct was to hit delete. Instead, her fingers began typing a reply.

"Who is this?" She could see the little green dot by the sender's profile picture, so the person was obviously still online.

There was a momentary pause, then the dancing dots started, signalling that the sender was typing a reply.

"It's William. William Steele. Sorry, I should have introduced myself first."

"Do I know you?" Alana began trawling her memory at warp speed – was it someone whom she had met at a Writers Workshop, or a book signing, perhaps? Steele? She only knew of one family with that surname. Surely not...

"It's been a long time since we last met. I know you from Castle Ridge."

A rock formed in Alana's stomach at the mere mention of Castle Ridge. That was a different time, a different life... But now the dialogue had been opened, she had to know more. She played along with the questioning, even though she was now ninety-nine per cent sure it was one of them.

"I'm sorry, I don't know anyone called William from Castle Ridge."

More dancing dots while William wrote his reply. Alana nervously tapped her fingers while she waited.

"It was twenty-five years ago. You were the girl in the car when my brother got killed..."

Bile rose in Alana's throat. The Castle Ridge ghosts of a former life had found her. Her hands began to shake while she tried to reply. Shouty-capitals seemed appropriate.

"WHY ARE YOU CONTACTING ME NOW!!!????"

"I'm sorry, Ms McQueen, I didn't mean to upset you. It's just that I saw you at the graveyard the other day. On the anniversary of Jon's death. I saw you lay a rose on his grave..."

So, there was someone there, someone watching me! Alana recalled the prickling sensation that she had felt on the back of her neck. Another message from William followed.

"I figured that you must still care. That's why I sent the flowers. To thank you for still caring..."

"So it was you who sent me the flowers?!!!"

"Yes."

A wave of guilt cursed through Alana as she pictured the bouquet in the dustbin. She considered her reply before typing. "It's a day that I will never forget."

"It's a day that I will never forget, either."

"I'm really sorry for the pain that it caused you and your family."

"Thanks. Time heals, but Jon's memory is always with me. He was my twin. It's our birthday today, by the way. We're thirty today."

Alana's eyes began filling with hot tears. A cry leaped from her throat, as the tears spilled over. She wiped her eyes so that she could see to type.

"I know that this is probably small comfort to you, William, but I will never forget what happened to your brother, and the pain that it caused your family. It is a pain that will go with me to my grave, believe me..."

"Thank you, Ms McQueen."

"By the way, William, you can call me Elaine. I think it's only fair that we separate Elaine from Alana if we're talking about the past." She paused before continuing her message. "Perhaps we can stay in touch now that you've found me."

"Yes, I'd like that."

"Quick question. Are you also WRS_85?"

"Yes."

Alana breathed a sigh of relief. "Well, I'd better get on with my work. Thanks for getting in touch, and thanks for the flowers. Hope it's okay to continue visiting Jon's grave? It would mean a lot to me. And happy birthday, BTW."

"Yes, of course you're welcome to still visit Jon. And who knows, maybe one day we'll meet..."

"Yes, maybe one day."

Alana disconnected the Messenger connection, then broke down and cried, years of suppressed tears, years of suppressed pain, all resurfaced with that one typed conversation.

After guiltily retrieving the limp remains of the bouquet out of the dustbin and arranging the surviving blooms in a little vase that she'd found under the sink, Alana made herself a relaxing cup of camomile tea. She settled herself into the corner of the sofa and tucked her legs up, all cocooned and cosy. The soothing herbs began working their magic, and Alana could finally feel the tension ease from her shoulders. She reflected on her message conversation with William Steele – even after all these years and a name change, the past has a habit of never letting go. And kudos to William for managing to track her down. But the accident which resulted in his brother's death could never be erased. She closed her eyes and allowed the memories of her bygone life in Castle Ridge to creep back to the forefront of her mind.

Mind's Eye

I am fourteen...

"My life back then had been nothing, and was going nowhere. As a youngster, I was the skinny, undernourished oddball. All the other kids seemed to have a proper best friend. But not me. Not when I was Elaine McCairn.

The only time I got any new and trendy clothing was when it came as a bagful of hand-me-downs from an older cousin. Not that she or my aunty ever visited. The bag was usually left on the back doorstep. No-one ever came to visit. And why was this? Because my piss-head parents thought more about booze and bingo than putting food on the table or clothes on my back. All these years, and my status was still very much quo. And what little money they had left over was used to pay off the never-never for things they couldn't really afford.

For a bright spark like me, it was too much – I knew that I was different. I wasn't blind, or stupid. And it hurt like hell – both physically from their beatings (yes, beatings had started by now), and emotionally from the school taunts. Parental resentment can be very painful, both physically as well as mentally. And it seemed the older I got, the worse it felt. Having a conscious understanding of rejection hurt in so many ways. Suicide had often been a consideration, but something deep inside always stopped me from taking that one step too far. Despite all this, I somehow managed to hang on to the dream of getting out of Castle Ridge and making a better life for myself. Maybe that's why I worked hard to get good grades. It would provide the future key to my escape.

This "escape" inspiration came from the most unusual of sources; every year, at the beginning of August, a travelling fun-fair rolled into town, and stayed for the week. The Castle Ridge Feast, we used to call it. It rejuvenated our little mining town with a welcome burst of colour, noise and energy. I loved going. Oh, the excitement that everyone felt when the first of the caravans and lorries started rolling in. Always the second Tuesday of August; they seemed to mysteriously appear overnight, and magically transform the Lodge Field with rides, food stalls and games. This was back in the day when it was considered exotic to win a coconut on the Coconut Shy! Strange how the arrival of the Feast also heralded the arrival of the darker nights. And it always rained!

All of the local kids would gravitate to this area and become a part of the energy. It was the place to hang out and look cool. I'd recently started a little pocket-money job delivering newspapers, so after years of being in a social no-man's-land, I could finally feel like a part of the crowd instead of a cash-strapped onlooker. Having my own money meant that I could now take care of myself – buy my own clothes and toiletries. I literally went from being the proverbial ugly duckling to an emerging swan. Older teens vied with each other for the top spot, posing around the edges of the rides, while giggling girls flirted with the fairground lads. Daring not to hold onto the motorbike handles on The Speedway ride. Boasting how many rides you could go on without throwing up! Even the catch-phrases stick with me: "Scream if you wanna go faster", and "When the red light flickers, hold onto your knickers!". The operators knew how to play to the crowd, and make the girls scream!

The Feast was very much a family occasion; there were plenty of rides to cater for all ages. I recall there being a beautifully painted mini-carousel for the kids, with little horses, and cars and motorbikes; and Hook-a-Duck, of course. But one of the favourite kiddie-rides was a little red train that went round and round in a circle, which meant that parents were obliged to wave every time their child went past. Maybe William and his twin brother enjoyed this ride, waving to their parents? Maybe I even saw them there? At least before...

The smells are still imprinted on my mind: toffee apples, hot-dogs and onions, candy floss. Sickly-sweet food aromas mixed with the smell of diesel from the lorry engines and generators that powered the rides and the lights. A colourful, sensory overload. And the caravans! All painted so beautifully! There was one caravan in particular which stood out from all the rest – one of those old-fashioned ones like a traditional gypsy caravan. It was a deep, dark red colour with gold paintwork. And the prettiest of lace curtains. How I dreamed of leaving home and becoming a part of the travelling fair; escaping from the life that I had. But would fairground life be any better? What would I be running away from? Did I really hate myself that much? No. It wasn't myself that I hated – it was my shit life.

I was worth more than Castle Ridge had to offer."

Chapter 17

So Near, Yet So...

Sunday 9th August, 2015

He ambled along the hawthorn hedgerows as he made his way back to the old hay barn. With surprisingly nimble fingers, he gently plucked the ripe wild blackberries and popped them into his little green tin, careful not to burst the delicate fruit. He'd had this tin for years, an old Golden Virginia rolling tobacco tin. Not that he had ever smoked; a disgusting habit, if ever there was one. But the tin, which he had found and utilised, was just the right size for his pocket. Not too big to be obtrusive and awkward, yet just the right size for a portion of berries or whatever he could forage. The blackberries had been good this summer, lucky for him. And the hawberries, ripe and red. Though he knew not to eat many of these; experience told him that he would get belly-ache if he ate too many. He had lived and learned as he went along, preferring to err on the side of caution. After all, it wasn't as though he could pop to the doctors or dentists like permanent folk.

He caught the faint, smoky whiff of a barbecue in the early evening air as he neared the cluster of tumble-down stone stables. His stomach rumbled, reminding him that he'd only eaten an ice-cream today, and that was due to the generosity of a toddler who had dropped it close to where he was resting. The hullabaloo of the little one crying had woken him from his snooze in the bushes behind the park bench, and piqued his curiosity. He always felt sad when he heard little ones crying, knowing that he would never have any of his own. But luckily for this particular toddler, his parents strolled with him back to the ice-cream kiosk, which gave the ever-hungry free-walker a golden opportunity to seize the dropped cone and whipped, creamy deliciousness. It even had a Flake...

Acutely aware that it would be difficult to cross the orchard unseen by the guests in the farmhouse garden, he settled down behind the old stables. He would just have to wait until twilight to get back to his barn, but at least he could pick up a few windfallen apples on the way. The farmer had once told him that he could stay on the farm providing he remained unseen, and didn't steal from them. He calculated that picking up windfalls didn't count as stealing, but were there for the taking. A calculation that had often saved him from near-starvation.

Not only did the evening breeze carry the tempting smells from the barbecue, it also carried the sound of a familiar laugh through the throng of voices and banter. Alana McQueen was visiting the farm – his Elaine! Butterflies rolled around in his stomach, pushing the hunger to one side. He needed a new game plan...

He scanned the orchard for a possible route through which he could sneak through the trees and long grass, in order to make it to the back of the tool shed and stone wall. A tool shed and stone wall which conveniently backed onto the garden area. He could be *that* close...

Jim Bullock flipped the chargrilled pork steaks and fat, juicy sausages with the practised ease of a man who loved to show off his barbecuing skills – particularly when he was in the company of a pretty visitor. And a well-known author, at that! There was no better way to advertise the quality of his meat than hosting regular barbecues for the locals. Mrs B joined the gathering, setting a colourful bowl of mixed salad, and some freshly made potato salad onto the outdoor table, before squeezing in next to Alana.

'Hurry up with that meat, Jim – we're all dying of starvation here!'

The farmer looked at his buxom wife, and laughed. 'I can see that,' he quipped, as he started placing the succulent offerings onto a large platter. 'Here you go, everyone. I don't want to be responsible for starvation rumours in town! Dig in...'

Mrs B lifted her can of cider into the air. 'Anyway, let's raise our bottles and cans to welcome back Alana... even if it's only for a short time,' she laughed. 'And for her bringing a touch of famousness to our humble table. Cheers!' She nodded in the direction of Alana, while everyone raised their drinks as a toast.

Alana could feel the heat rising in her cheeks at the "famous" tag – something which never sat well with her. 'Thanks, Mrs B.'

One of the barbecue guests, who was already becoming well soaked with Stella Artois, loudly raised a question towards their esteemed guest. 'Oh, so you're not back here permanently, then? How long are you here for?'

'Just until Friday 28th. I'm on a deadline for my next book, plus I want to get back to Manchester before the Peak gets invaded by Bank Holiday tourists...'

A murmur of agreement rippled around the table of locals, all being well versed in the feeling of being overrun on hot days and holidays.

After politely fending off numerous other questions about writing and her next book, Alana managed to engage Mrs B in some surreptitious questioning of her own. She absently toyed with her meat while she spoke.

'You know you were telling me about that tramp the other day – the day we went shopping – you mentioned that he'd been in these parts for a long time, and that he was no bother to the locals...'

Mrs B shrugged, and nodded as she took a swig of cider to wash down her food before replying. 'S'right. Never been a bit o'bother. Jim once had a word with him; told him never to steal from us, and never light any fires. And, of course, to keep out of our way. He's pretty much kept to that. We very rarely see him, perhaps only in the evening shadows.'

Alana's eyes widened. 'But doesn't it bother you – someone freeloading on your generosity, I mean?'

'Not really. I'd rather do this than find him frozen to death in the bottom of the hedgerow...'

Alana pondered Mrs B's reasoning. 'True. I can understand that. But all the same, having someone skulking around on your property. Don't you think it's a bit, well, creepy? He could be watching you...'

Mrs B self-looked up and down her voluptuous, Rubenesque torso, and giggled. 'Well, not unless he's into fat ladies! Why do you ask?'

'Well, it's just that I get the feeling that someone's watching me from the garden. And then on Friday, when I got back from shopping, some of my, erm... my underwear had gone missing from the washing line...' Alana held her head low and downcast to avoid looking directly at Mrs B.

A burst of laughter from her table partner was not what she was expecting. 'Really?! I don't think that our old tramp would be into stealing underwear. Food, maybe, but not lingerie... No, love, I can't imagine that he would do something like that.'

'But... And there's been other strange things, too. Like someone leaving a rose on the doorstep, and, and, a dead cat!' She kept her voice low so that the other guests wouldn't hear.

'A dead cat!' Mrs B's reply was much louder than Alana would have liked, drawing uninvited comments and opinions into the conversation.

Being wise to the feral world of his barn-mousers, Farmer Jim took up the thread. 'Honestly, love – if you've got dead cats on your doorstep, it's most likely one of our old ones that's gone away to die. Especially if they've chewed on a poisoned mouse. I wouldn't worry too much about it, lass.'

'But, it had a—' She was going to add "tag around its neck", but Jim inadvertently cut her off.

'—Anyway, who's for dessert? I think it's time for apple pie and ice-cream!'

Alana's stomach really couldn't face the thought of more food on top of the stress knot that had formed. Why was no-one taking all this seriously? More fool her for having thrown everything in the dustbin and deleting the photos. That would have proved that she wasn't lying! That she wasn't imagining things!

From his aural vantage point, he could hear the hum and rise of conversation, and the tones of Alana's voice. On the one hand, she sounded different – more mature and educated. But on the other, she still sounded like his old Elaine – nervous and slightly on edge. And from what he could make out, was less than complimentary about his unseen presence, even though the farmer's wife had tried to reassure her that the "tramp was harmless". Tramp! Why do people still use that derogatory term? He was a free-walker! Free to come and go as he pleased. Free to walk wherever he pleased. Free!

He tuned in to the voices saying their goodbyes, and their thanks for a lovely evening. That they must do it again, sometime. He adjusted his position so that he would be able to creep along the hedgerow, invisible in the evening shadows, and follow Alana back to the cottage.

After all, he had to make sure that his girl got home safely.

Chapter 18

Airing Dirty Laundry

Monday 10th August, 2015

Anger gnawed away in his stomach, causing the cold sausage that he'd had for breakfast to rise with the bile and sting the back of his throat. He always felt irked when he saw other men down at the cottage, near his girl. After surreptitiously "accompanying" Alana home from the barbecue last night, he had returned to the hay barn to find a wrapped plate of barbecue left-overs and a bottle of beer waiting by the door for him. He had eagerly taken the food – there was enough to last him almost a week by his standards – but left the beer behind. A strong sense of self-pride for having quit the deadly booze habit meant that he could still hold his head high and refrain from taking freebies. But food – that was never refused.

He narrowed his eyes as he refocused the binoculars for a better view of what was happening. It looked like some kind of installation work was being carried out. Cameras! They were having security cameras installed!

Fuck!

His mind went into frustrated overdrive. In which direction were the cameras pointing? What was the spread of the lens? He mentally tried to calculate the angle and distance, but it was no good from this vantage point. He would have to get closer to stand any chance of working it out.

Damn! Damn! Damn!

Maybe he'd overdone it a little. Overstepped the mark. He'd obviously frightened his love. But that hadn't been his intention – he'd only wanted to leave gifts; tokens of his affection. He'd only wanted to make sure that she was coming to no harm. Well, if that was their game, then he would just have to play along.

He could *do* sneaky.

He could *do* subterfuge.

He could *do* whatever the hell he liked...

***

'Wishee-Washee's Laundry Service...' Jack held the bag of clean towels and bedding in front of his face and laughed when Alana opened the door.

She played along with his joke. 'And about time, too! I hope it's fresh and clean, and soft and fluffy!'

'Yes, ma'am...'

Alana stepped to one side, and offered Jack to come in with the change of bedding, towels and tea-towels. 'I didn't realise that you would come to do this. I thought I would be stuck with the same stuff for a month.'

'Nope – it's been two weeks, so time for a change. We only provide the best service, you know!' he teased.

'Great. Won't you stop for a coffee while I get the dirty laundry together for you?'

'Sounds good. In fact, I'll go and make it while you gather up the stuff. Still the same – white with no sugar?'

'You remembered. I'm impressed.' Alana chuckled, then continued, 'And seeing as how this is your house, I don't need to tell you where things are!'

Once Alana had bagged up the dirty laundry, she brought the bag into the kitchen and dropped it by the door, before sitting down.

'There you go, Jack. All sorted.'

'Thanks. So, how have you been since the cat and the phantom knicker-nicker incidents? Your mood seems a bit lighter today.' Jack set Alana's coffee mug in front of her, then took a seat opposite. 'Any more signs of prowlers or tramps in the garden?' He watched her closely for any indication of agitation – Olivia was still convinced that Alana had made up the stories just to keep him at her beck and call.

Alana's mood flipped in an instant, and she shot him a sharp glance. 'It's not funny, Jack! How would you feel if this had happened in your garden? What if someone had helped themselves to some of Olivia's underwear? I even felt a presence last night when I was walking home from the farm.'

'From the farm?'

'Yes, I went there last night. To a barbecue. Apparently there's an old tramp who lives in the area, although they maintain that he's harmless. I still felt uncomfortable walking home, though.'

'A tramp? Look, maybe it's all–'

'–In my mind. No, Jack. No, it isn't. I know what I've seen. What I've experienced...'

Jack's voice rose in exasperation. 'Okay! Okay! I get your point. You could still report these happenings to the police, you know. Then at least they'll have something on record. Maybe we could ask them to do the odd drive-by? Show their presence a little more.'

'I've told you before, Jack – I haven't been directly approached or threatened in any way. I haven't actually *seen* anyone. So I can hardly envisage them wasting time driving up and down the lane every now and again.'

He held his hands up in defeat. 'Well, at least we now have the security cameras – I can see that the alarm company has installed them, as promised.'

'Yes, the guy came first thing this morning.' Alana softened a little, and sighed. 'I know you find all this a little *too* fictional, a little too over the top. But thanks for taking my concerns seriously – I feel more at ease now.' She picked up her phone. 'Here, look – there's an app that you can download, then you have access to the cameras, just as I do.' After a few taps, her phone screen suddenly showed a black and white image of the back patio and a part of the lawn from *Camera 1*, then flipped to an equally grainy view of the front doorstep, path and dustbin from *Camera 2*. 'All very clever!'

Jack nodded, impressed, then began fiddling with his phone. Alana moved closer to him, her hand catching his as she helped him select the correct settings. She could feel the heat from his breath, and smell his clean sandalwood fragrance, as she guided him through the set-up process. This was not the way that she was supposed to feel. She was too close. She briefly zoned out, only brought back to the present moment by the clatter of her empty coffee mug being knocked over onto the floor.

'Phew, that was lucky – it didn't break! Anyway, there you go, the app is all set up for you...' A few seconds of empty, awkward silence ticked by while Alana readjusted her mental demeanour.

Jack picked up on the momentary tension. He looked for something with which to redirect the conversation, and spotted the remnants of Will's bouquet in a little vase.

'Pretty flowers. From an admirer?' He tried to make it sound lighthearted, teasing.

'They're from Will. William Steele...'

Jack frowned. 'The Steeles from Castle Ridge? Why would they be sending you flowers?' The hairs on his forearms bristled, knowing the history that Alana had with this family.

'Will's the twin brother of little Jon... He, erm... He saw me at the cemetery the other day. And, erm, he figured out who I was. Anyway, he tracked me down, and sent me some flowers to say thank-you. For still caring.' Knowing that this had been a bone of contention over the years, Alana kept her head down in order to avoid Jack's glare.

'But I thought you weren't going to go there anymore? We've talked about this many times, remember. You have to let go of the past, Alana. You can't keep dwelling on the accident – it's a sure-fire way of heading for–'

'–Another breakdown... I know exactly what you're going to say. And yes, I know there's a risk. But it was the twenty-fifth anniversary. I felt compelled to mark it in some way.' She looked up, and locked his gaze. 'Just this last time. I promise...'

'I hope so, Alana. You have a great life, and a great career. You're about to launch your next book. There's no reason to keep dwelling on the past. Let it go.'

'You're right, Jack. As always. Now, let's change the subject–' She smiled, giving herself a few precious seconds to find a new topic of conversation. Now would not be a good time to tell Jack that she and Will had recently opened up a friendly line of conversation on Messenger.

Chapter 19

Disconnected From the Past

Tuesday 11th August, 2015

'So, what's really going on, Jack? Why are you constantly jumping to help Alana? I could have taken the clean laundry. It's just one thing after another...' Olivia banged her fist down hard onto the dining table, causing the plates and cutlery to jump and clatter.

'I was only taking clean laundry, for God's sake!' he defended. 'It's the two-week swap-over point...'

But Olivia wasn't listening. 'What *is* this hold that she's got over you? You're married to me, in case you've forgotten!'

Jack began grinding his teeth, and took a deep breath. 'I'm really sorry, Liv. Yes, I know I'm no longer married to her. Alana and I divorced over five years ago, and you know it! But I can't help but feel protective of her, especially with all that's been happening recently.'

Olivia blushed and sighed, afraid that she'd overstepped the mark in her frustration. She began serving the lasagne and salad onto their plates to cover her embarrassment.

'You know that she had bouts of depression and a breakdown, right?' Jack paused for a moment while he uncorked the accompanying bottle of red wine, the cork sliding out with a resounding *pop*. Out of respect for his ex-wife's privacy, Jack had always refrained from divulging too much information, but he knew the moment had come to finally reveal more about Alana's past.

Olivia nodded, and pushed her glass towards him.

'There were years of guilt and self-loathing that led to that breakdown. When Alana was about seventeen or eighteen, she and her boyfriend were out for a Sunday drive around the back lanes where they used to live, over in Castle Ridge – you know, the place with the castle on the hill. Anyway, this kid – a little boy – just ran out from behind a parked ice-cream van, and straight in front of her boyfriend's car. Apparently the impact wasn't that hard – there were enough witnesses to absolve them of any reckless driving or speeding. It literally was the wrong place at the wrong time, both for them and for the little boy. But he landed awkwardly, and somehow hit his head on the edge of the pavement. Despite everyone's best efforts, the little boy died.' Jack looked at Olivia, and saw that she had tears welling in her eyes.

'I'm sorry... I never realised that she'd been through such a trauma... You've never really talked about it before.'

'As you can imagine, the Castle Ridge gossip-machine soon started badmouthing the tragedy, and in the end she and her boyfriend split up. There was just so much pressure on them. She could never shake off the feeling that people were talking about her behind her back and pointing the finger of blame. So she moved away, over here to the Peak, and tried to put it all behind her. There was nothing to keep her in Castle Ridge – her parents were a couple of abusive piss-heads from all accounts, who drank their way to an early grave. Alana preferred not to talk about her childhood...'

'Does she have any siblings?'

Jack shook his head.

'What about grandparents? Aunties and uncles?'

'Yes, she had grandparents, and one aunty, I think, but they never really got involved. To be honest, I think they were too afraid to report them. The authorities would have probably put Alana into care.'

'But surely that would have been more preferable than living in dire conditions?' Olivia shivered and rubbed her arms, her body language now oozing genuine concern for her husband's ex.

'You would think so,' agreed Jack. 'But that doesn't always make people feel comfortable with reporting such a situation...'

'Poor thing. So she's been quite the lone-wolf...'

'Yep.' Jack poked around at his meal, then put down his fork. 'It didn't help her frame of mind either, when she heard that the child's mother committed suicide a few years later, unable to get over the loss. It was all this chaos and pain in her younger life that made Alana re-evaluate her own direction – she knew that she was worth more.'

'Oh, that's awful. So much tragedy...' Olivia took a moment to process the newly gleaned information. 'Is that why she never learned to drive? Because of the accident?'

Jack nodded. 'She hates being in a car, especially in the front seat. She would rather catch a bus, or walk, than be in a car. Holidays and travel were always a bit of a sticking point for us.'

Olivia mentally recalled Alana's nervousness at getting into the car when they went out to the quiz night at the beginning of her stay. And that had been as a back-seat passenger. 'It must have been difficult living at the cottage, then? It's quite a long walk up and down the lane to get to the town.'

'Not so difficult. Luckily she enjoys fresh air and exercise – that's why she took up jogging, and I bought her a mountain bike.'

Olivia picked up the wine to replenish her glass, and top up Jack's, as an unspoken indicator for him to continue. There was so much that she never knew or realised about Alana's past.

'Thanks,' acknowledged Jack, grateful for the relaxing effect that the wine was having on him. It helped to blanket the guilt that he felt talking so candidly about his ex-wife. 'She spent years on antidepressants and sleeping tablets. And psycho-therapy, or whatever it's called. Anything to try and get rid of the guilt and bad dreams. To this day, I don't think she's forgiven herself for what happened. It's something that she's re-lived countless times.' He looked at Olivia, his face soft and sympathetic. 'Who wouldn't have had a breakdown...?'

'Is she still taking any kind of medication?'

Jack shrugged noncommittally. 'I'm not sure, to be honest. That's her business.'

'So how did she become a writer?' Olivia asked, still curious to know more about Jack's ex. In all the time they'd been married, this was the most that he'd opened up about his first wife.

'It was just another way of keeping her mind busy – help to keep it focused while letting it have some freedom. She spotted some adult-education classes for Criminology, English, and Creative Writing, so immersed herself in college. She found that she had a talent for writing, and that's how it all started. She could expel the dark thoughts into her work, so to speak. Anyway, as time went on, she managed to get an agent and a publishing deal.'

'And build quite a successful career... She's quite well known, isn't she – has quite a devoted fan base around this area?'

'True,' acknowledged Jack. 'Not that she likes the spotlight. She prefers to hide behind her words. That's why she's always written under a pen-name: Alana McQueen. Created a new persona. It was her way of protecting her former identity and burying the past. Her reality became a blur, and just melded into the world that she created in her head. She couldn't separate the two.'

Olivia's eyes widened, taken aback. 'So, Alana McQueen isn't her real name?'

Jack shrugged, and pushed his plate away. 'It might as well be. I can't remember when she last used her real name, apart from on official documents.'

She couldn't resist fishing for more titbits. 'So what about when you were married – didn't she take your surname, Adams, as I did?'

Jack neither confirmed nor denied, just left it open-ended. 'Like I said, she's always used Alana McQueen.'

The atmosphere and conversation stilled for a moment, as Jack and Olivia each became absorbed in their own thoughts. Olivia rolled the elegant stem of the wine glass between her fingers, while more questions formulated in her mind.

'I know this is a deeply personal question, Jack, but is that why you never had any kids? Because of her mental state?'

Jack's cheeks flushed slightly. 'Yes, partly. But also because she was afraid of being a bad parent herself. Too many bad memories of her own childhood – she didn't want to risk passing on any bad genes. She was quite literally embarrassed of her own parents.'

Olivia thought about her own privileged, only-child upbringing: happy parents, a nice home, her own pony – she could only look back on her childhood with a sense of pride. Armed with all this new and thought-provoking information about her husband's ex, she put her hands over Jack's, and gave him a weak smile. 'I'm sorry for being so harsh and judgemental.'

'It's okay – you weren't to know. It isn't exactly something that either Alana or I shout about.' He gave Olivia a wan smile. 'What with this stalker thing, then finding a dead cat on the doorstep – *and* I've just found out that she's been to visit the graveyard. It would be enough to tip anyone over the edge! Maybe you now understand why I'm so worried about her.' He looked at Olivia, his gaze fixed and harsh. A look that said the discussion was for this moment only, and never to be repeated.

Realising that she was on sketchy ground if she put too much pressure on either Jack or Alana to cool things a little, especially after the recent events over at the cottage, Olivia sighed and paused while she sought to find the right words and tone of voice, before continuing. She endeavoured to look and sound genuinely compassionate. 'But what can we do? She's clearly not comfortable being here. Why don't you try and speak to her – maybe get her to cut short the booking? Or maybe speak to her agent? I would much rather give a refund to Alana, than her being unhappy here.'

Jack toyed with his napkin, his mind torn between the two women in his life. 'I really don't know what to do, Olivia. I really don't know...'

Mind's Eye

I am seventeen...

"But then my life changed in the blink of an eye. I was in the wrong place at the wrong time, as was Jon Steele. And he paid the ultimate price.

I still re-live the moment of the impact – it plays like a loop in my mind; the dull thud as his little body hit the front of the car, the screams of the witnesses, the screams of the child's mother, and the chaos that ensued. The look on young Will's face as his father tried to shield him from the tragedy – the tragedy which took his brother's life. His twin brother. If only he, or we, had been a few seconds earlier or later, maybe the moment would have been avoided...

We'd been out cruising around the country lanes, and spotted the ice-cream van as we approached from the opposite direction. It was a beautiful sunny day – the perfect day for an ice-cream. So we started slowing down with the intention of pulling up to grab a Sunday afternoon treat.

And that's when it happened. This little kid just ran out from behind the ice-cream van, and...

My boyfriend, Steve, just sat – stunned – gripping the steering wheel, his knuckles white. I recall someone trying to help him out of the car but they were unable to loosen his grip; it was as if he was frozen to the spot, rigid with fear. And I remember trying to scream, but nothing would come out. Everything *became muffled, and for long moments, life moved in slow motion.*

Surreal. Slow-mo...

Shocking. Slow-mo...

Even though the accident was declared just that – we were absolved of any wrong-doing – the acid tongues of the gossips soon began spitting their venom. Castle Ridge is a small mining town, and the little boy's family was well known and well respected in the local community. Although I didn't know them personally, I knew of them. The boy's mother had a hairdressing salon, and her parents were also local business people – her mother had the local fruit-and-veg shop, and her father was a solicitor. They had connections everywhere. Steve and I were made to feel like murderous criminals. Just when I had been getting my life on some kind of track, it was completely derailed.

For a while, we both turned to drink, and wild living. It helped to block out the memories. But in the end, it just pushed us apart – he continued down the booze-route, but I was afraid of ending up like my parents. If that's what alcoholism looked like, then I didn't want to be a part of it – the lost hours and days; feeling like shit. I decided to take charge of my life, and get out of Castle Ridge.

It was time for a fresh start."

Chapter 20

Burning With Curiosity

Wednesday 12th August, 2015

Unable to get last night's conversation about Alana out of her mind, Olivia put the mood board and swatch of fabrics to one side. The focus just wasn't there, and the last thing she wanted to do was make a design faux-pas for the Johnsons; they mixed in wealthy circles and could be the gateway to more commissions if she managed to achieve the right *look* for their new barn conversion. They wanted a practical country-style with a modern, bold twist, which perfectly aligned with this year's design trends: an eclectic mix of earthy reds, statement prints and textures, and opulent lamps. She sighed, temporarily defeated.

The deeper their discussion had gone, the more Olivia wanted to know about Jack's ex-wife. On the surface, Alana seemed like a lovely woman – she hadn't been a bother to them; not at all vengeful, unlike some ex-wife stories that she'd heard. But the real Alana, the one deep within, sounded like a whimpering child with a dark story to tell. It was as though she projected one persona to her public, but quite another behind closed doors. Olivia recalled the stinging, narrow-eyed look that

Jack had given her as their dinner conversation drew to a close – a look that said the information was supposed to stay within those four walls. But her curiosity had been aroused, and she knew that her work-day and creativity wouldn't return until she'd been to visit Alana. Although, her name wasn't really Alana. So who the hell was she, then? Jack never said. That settled it – she would pick up two large cappuccinos *to-go*, and a couple of pastry treats from the coffee shop in Buxton, then stop off at the High Peak Bookstore on the way to the cottage to get the latest copy of *Derbyshire Life* magazine for Alana.

Have some cosy girl-time...

***

The hairs bristled on the back of Alana's neck as she caught sight of Olivia's shiny new Prius pulling up in front of the cottage.

What does the eco-warrior want? She rolled her eyes, and tut-tutted. *Trying to save the planet one Prius at a time while encouraging clients to buy the next "must-have" in design trends. Double standards...*

Alana noticed that Olivia was carrying a take-out tray of coffee and bakes. A sudden mind-image of the wicked witch in Snow White, with the basket of poisoned apples, manifested itself, causing a wry smile. She rearranged her demeanour to one of a welcoming friend rather than a defensive ex, and quickly gave the sitting room a once-over, plumping cushions, and making sure that everything was neat and aligned. Should she go to the door ready for the knock, or wait for the knock then go to the door? She opted for the latter, not wanting to look too eager. But *why* was she here? She steeled herself for an uncomfortable coffee-date.

***

After a tortuous couple of hours of inane, and at times forced chit-chat, Alana found a natural break in which to smile sweetly and make her excuses in order to bring their "get to know each other better girl-time" (as Olivia had called it), to a close. Apart from Jack, they really didn't have anything in common. She had sensed that much of Olivia's questioning was nothing more than digging for dirt on her life, followed by bouts of fake sympathy. But no worries – Alana had countered Olivia's dirt-digging by consciously allowing the odd "slip of the tongue" with faux-snippets about her life with Jack. Alana smiled to herself. Sometimes one needed to release the primal instinct of appearing stronger than the opponent! Ha! That would give wife #2 something to think about...

She looked around the sitting room area and sighed at the mess. Flaky pastry crumbs and coffee-cup rings decorated the coffee table, while crumpled cushions irritated her zen. The hot-pink lipstick residue which graced Olivia's take-out cup glared at Alana, taunting her with its vibrancy. In her mind's eye, she could see the lipstick moving, starting to form words of revenge; words that told her she'd made an almighty fuck-up of her life. A rush of adrenaline flooded her stomach, while tuneless hollow voices echoed around her mind. No-one wanted her because she wasn't worthy.

Right from being a kid...

Worthless.

A worthless person.

A worthless wife.

A worthless author.

A worthless life.

A worthless piece of shit.

She meant nothing. Her words meant nothing. She could feel her pulse starting to race, causing a thudding sensation in her temples. The thudding merged in her frontal lobe, pounding a rhythmic beat with the hissed mind-taunting:

Worthlessss.

Worthlessss.

Worthlessss.

She snatched up her phone and searched Jack's number, not giving him a chance to speak when the call connected.

'Why did you send her over? Did you send her to spy on me?'

Caught off guard, Jack spluttered his response. 'Alana, I've no idea who or what you're talking about...'

'Oliva, of course!'

'Olivia?'

'Oh, don't sound so surprised, Jack. Yes, Olivia. She came by for a visit today, acting all nicey-nicey, bringing coffee and cakes. I'm supposed to be here working. This is *my* space for the month. Does she drop by and have coffee with all of your bookings?'

Jack's mind raced as he absorbed Alana's screeched information, his reply curt. 'One: I didn't know that Olivia was planning to come and visit you. And two: this is a bit different – it isn't like you're a stranger to her!'

'Well, I'm sorry, but I think it's a bit creepy. I came here to get some peace and quiet so that I could work – get out of the city, get away from the phone and visitors. And what happens? All manner of things, that's what!'

Jack sighed – he could now understand Olivia's concerns during last night's discussion. He took a deep breath. 'You could always cut short your retreat, and we'll give you a refund. It *is* an option, you know. You don't have to stay.'

But Alana wasn't listening. Her mind had blanked any incoming conversation and had started supplying her with its own information. '... Dead animals, random flowers, cryptic messages... And people creeping around in the garden... What kind of place is this? This isn't the cottage that I remember. This isn't the peaceful haven you describe it as...'

Jack's pulse began to race, causing an icy feeling in his veins. 'In all honesty, Alana, I don't know how those things happened. You're so well thought of locally that anyone could have sent you those flowers. Stop making everything seem so sinister.' He immediately regretted his words, knowing that Alana would probably now start analysing the villagers. 'Why don't you go to the police if you have concerns about your safety?'

'Because no-one has made a direct approach towards me. No-one has made a direct threat. That's how it works, Jack.'

'Well, at least keep a documented note of things – jot down all the occurrences. Just in case...'

His words were swallowed up and stomped on, Alana's tirade continuing. '...And now you send your wife to check up on me!'

'I did not!'

'You really expect me to believe that!'

'Yes, I do! Look, Alana, stop dumping all your emotional crap on me! You pushed me away, remember. I've moved on. You need to do the same. Move on from the past, let it go. It can't be changed.'

'How can I let it go? It's still following me, tearing down the walls that I'd built up. I'm losing my mind, Jack...' Alana cracked, her voice giving way to sobs. 'I'm sorry, Jack. Sorry for bothering you again in your nice life...' She disconnected the call, cutting off Jack's words as he tried to reply.

Jack stared at the phone, then began scrolling through to find Olivia's number. How could she have been so stupid! His thumb hesitated over the green-telephone icon. No – this was something that needed a face-to-face discussion. But not yet. He was way too angry to face Olivia. Women! He opted instead to send a message. "Got to work late tonight. Don't wait up." His phone pinged seconds later with a thumbs-up. Jack threw his phone down onto his desk, and massaged his eyes. This day was not going well.

Chapter 21

More Than She Bargained For

Wednesday 12th August, 2015

Unable to drive any further, Olivia pulled the Prius into a farm layby and wound down the window before turning off the engine. She closed her eyes, and allowed the calming sounds and fresh air of the countryside to envelop her senses while she tried to steady her nerves.

Had it been a mistake to visit Alana? She was only trying to be nice – trying to know and understand the woman that her husband was once married to. A very broken woman.

On the outside, Alana took pride in her appearance; she was always neatly dressed, even when casual. Her mussed-up yet styled hair looked effortless, and she wore just enough make-up to enhance her natural prettiness. Olivia looked at her fingernails – French-manicured, neat and precise. But fake. Just like her eyelashes, her tan, and her highly-groomed appearance. All fake. In essence, she was no better than Alana; creating and maintaining a fake persona was hard work. Why was it impossible to just be yourself? To be comfy with who you really are?

She recalled Jack once telling her that Alana was a neat-freak – everything had to be in its place, all tidy and organised, almost to the point of obsession. Daily life was governed by sticky-notes of "to-do" lists, all neatly written, then crossed through when each task had been completed. She had even employed a cleaner once a week when she lived at the cottage to help keep things spit-spot. Presumably this was a throw-back from living in a shit-tip as a child – a complete reversal of what she'd been brought up in. A way to escape the mental dirt of a former life. Even the cottage, though no longer Alana's home, still looked orderly and tidy when she'd turned up unannounced today. And Olivia was pretty sure that the cushions had been re-plumped while she had nipped to the bathroom for a pee.

One thing that was particularly gnawing at Olivia though, was the way that Alana had portrayed Jack while they were married. Yes, at first he had been Mr Helpful, Mr Nice-guy. The knight in shining armour who had rescued her from a fall, both literally and metaphorically. But then the sniping comments had begun. Why couldn't she get out of bed? Why couldn't she do this? Why couldn't she do that? She needed to pull herself together. He was always looking for ways to pick a fight – and yes, he had slapped her occasionally. Even when they'd been out to any of his work-related events, or her promotional author events, he'd practically told her what to wear, and how to look. He had manipulated her shyness to ensure she stayed quiet, thereby making him look like the doting husband. The perfect cover to his behind-closed-doors behaviour.

Was this really the Jack that she was married to?

Yes, they'd had a few arguments over the years, but don't all married couples have disagreements? And it was her own choice to look nice for Jack – wasn't it? Or had he surreptitiously encouraged the fakeness that she was now accustomed to? After all, she was ten years his junior – a prize catch, or "arm-candy", as one of his work colleagues had once called her. Her mind whirred with memories and scenarios from hers and Jack's relationship. Was it as mutual as she thought? Or...?

Jack had sounded so convincing with all the stories that he had told her about Alana's illnesses, and their life together. He sounded like a genuinely caring husband – not at all the way in which Alana had portrayed him today.

And now here she was, back in their life, and Jack was jumping to her needs. Olivia's mind began analysing the reasons for Jack's sudden attentiveness towards his ex-wife. Maybe he was deliberately being nice to Alana so that she wouldn't spill the real beans about their marriage. But if he had been such a monster, why would she bother coming to stay at the cottage? Was it some kind of calculated revenge? It just didn't make any sense. And all these strange, stalker-like happenings at the cottage? Was Jack behind it, exacting some kind of mind-game to tip Alana over the edge? She was, after all, fragile to say the least. But what would he have to gain from doing this? Alana was fully independent of him. She rapped her fingertips on the steering wheel, agitated.

Olivia looked at her watch, surprised by how long she'd been parked up in the lay-by. Armed with this new information about her husband, butterflies tickled her stomach at the very thought of going home.

Maybe Alana had been spinning stories...?

Olivia rather hoped so.

Her phone pinged with an incoming message – it was from Jack. "Got to work late tonight. Don't wait up." A loud, involuntary sigh of relief escaped from Olivia. She replied with a simple "thumbs-up" emoji.

Mind's Eye

Escape: A new life begins

"It was the greatest, mind-freeing moment – packing my bags with what few personal possessions I wanted to take with me – and saying "fuck-you" to the people and life of Castle Ridge.

Don't get me wrong – I know that I'm painting such a tainted image – but when you're eighteen, and have just spent the past year being the focus of unwarranted gossip, you feel like everyone and everything is against you. Though I was just as much a victim of the tragedy, I was made to feel like the antagonist. That's how it felt at the time.

And so I headed for the rolling hills and dales of the Derbyshire Peak District. Somewhere that was as calming as it was beautiful. Finding a job was quite easy – in fact, I ended up with two jobs for a while. During the daytime, I worked in a little bookshop, then a pub in the evening. I managed to find a poky little bedsit over one of the shops in the village, and began rebuilding my life. Books became my friends – I could read and read, and escape to so many different places. I also took the decision to become teetotal, which seems a bit of an oxymoron when working in a pub – but I had seen first-hand the damage that booze can cause; not only for those who drink themselves into oblivion, but the loved ones who have to stand by and suffer their actions.

This new-found love affair with books deepened even further after enrolling on some adult education courses at the local college. My good grades from school stood me in good stead so that I could get onto the courses that interested me. And, of course, I had a good study ethic, so made the most of every lesson. The Creative Writing classes opened up such a whole new world for me – now I no longer had to read about these fictional places and lives, but could create them for myself! It was such a mind-cleansing release. My written work won a few local prizes, and set me on a path to becoming Alana McQueen. It was the perfect opportunity to reinvent myself completely.

Being at college during the daytime meant that I had to give up the job in the bookshop during the week, but I still liked to help out at weekends. The pub offered me a few more evening hours, which helped to compensate financially, and life took on a routined balance between college, work and writing. Imagine my joy when my first novel was nominated for a debut-author's crime writer award! It was the confidence boost that I needed, and confirmed that by nurturing self-trust, I could achieve anything. Although I had published this first novel independently, the award meant that my work began receiving more interest, and led to getting an agent and a publishing deal. I know that this is a hard-fought dream for many authors, but maybe I was in the right place at the right time.

And just when I thought that life couldn't get any better, I met Jack. I quite literally fell for him outside of his office door, when I slipped on some ice. Being the gent that he is, he took care of me at the hospital, and our relationship just blossomed from there.

It sounds like the stuff that fairytales are made from – and for a while, it was.

But unlike most fairytales, ours didn't have a happy ending..."

Chapter 22

Storm Clouds

Thursday 13th August, 2015

Olivia sensed that Jack's mood was as dark and taut as her own as she watched him come down the open-plan stairs, his silhouette backlit by the full-height window. Grey clouds gathered beyond, adding to the already sombre air. This was one of the first times that they'd consciously slept apart since being married, except for when she'd been on "sourcing" trips, or Jack on business trips. He looked rough, unshaven. She'd heard him come in around 1am – very late for "working late at the office". But instead of quietly slipping into bed beside her, he'd chosen to sleep in the spare room. Alarm bells naturally went off in Olivia's mind, making sleep impossible.

Jack scowled at her as he sat down at the opposite side of the breakfast island, causing a wave of anxiety-adrenaline to flood her system. Olivia took a deep breath and waited. He should be the one to speak first; surely a night in the spare room must mean that he's the one with a guilty conscience? She held her ground.

'You stupid, stupid bitch!' He paused, and glared intently at Olivia. This was not the opening line that she'd expected. 'Of all the stupid fucking things to do, you had to go and visit Alana. You just couldn't keep your nose out, could you!'

Words froze in Olivia's brain. She blinked to hold back the involuntary tears that were forming.

'All that I told you at dinner the other evening, I told you in confidence. But, no – you had to go and stick your nose into Alana's business, into Alana's life...' He stood up, and raised his hand ready to point an accusatory finger – a gesture which caused an auto-flinch reaction in Olivia. She let out an involuntary gasp, and put her arms up to shield her face.

'Really? Really? Did you really think that I was going to hit you!' His expression turned from one of anger to shock.

'If you lay one finger on me, Jack Adams, I will walk straight out of that door...'

He sat back down, and caught his breath, trying to even the rhythm of his pulse. Olivia broke the tense silence.

'Yes, I went to visit Alana yesterday. I admit that I was curious to know more about her. About her life, and childhood, and what makes her tick. And yes, I'm probably even a little jealous of the hold that she still has over you. Is that so wrong?' Olivia glared at him, her gaze hard and challenging.

'Olivia, I've never hid any of the reasons why I've been to the cottage to help Alana. Every reason has been genuine. I would have done the same if it had been a regular Airbnb guest.' He paused to take a drink of his coffee, and let the caffeine work its magic. 'She called me at work yesterday, *SCREAMING* at me – saying that I'd sent you to check up on her. Screaming about everything that's ever gone wrong in her life. I've had it up to here with both of you!' He slapped the front of his forehead to indicate that he was maxed out with the women in his life. His voice rose in intensity. 'Just keep out of things that don't concern you. Let her finish her time here in peace, and she'll be on her way...'

A million and one thoughts raced around Olivia's mind, but her mouth overtook her brain, causing her to spew out words that, once out, could never be retrieved. 'Did you ever hit Alana?'

Jack stopped dead all movement and stared at Olivia, eyes wide. He struggled to find any coherent reply.

Olivia seized the opportunity to continue. 'She said that you manipulated her illness so that she had to depend on you. That you used to control her. And that you hit her...'

'And what do you think? Look at me. Look at the man in front of you, Olivia. What do you think?'

'I... I... No, Jack. No, I don't think you're capable of those things. But the way she talked about the manipulation. It sounded convincing. I admit to being a little scared...'

Jack sighed, and rubbed the stubble on his jawline. 'No, I'm not the manipulator here – she is. When she starts rolling with things – with her illness, it can create delusions. And once she gets something fixed in her mind, then it all becomes very real. Look at the cat-thing – we'll never know for sure whether that was real, or not. It's the same with this, Liv. I *promise* you.' He reached over and put his hands over hers. 'I've only ever told you the truth. I was her carer, not her abuser.'

Tears filled Olivia's eyes and spilled over, and for a few moments she found it difficult to speak. 'Delusions?'

'Yes, delusions. And her depression, and obsessive behaviour. It's a throwback to her childhood. To all the trauma.' He looked at his wife, his eyes flat and dark, framed by puffy half circles; a testimony to his tiredness.

'I'm so sorry, Jack! I'm so very sorry for having believed her. I guess she just made me feel insecure.'

'You have no reason to feel insecure, Liv. I would never do anything to hurt you.' Jack went around to his wife and encircled her in his arms, then searched out her face with kisses. 'Come here, you silly girl.' He wiped the mascara smudges from under her eyes. 'And don't worry – I'll be having some very strong words with Alana about this. C'mon, we've got a lost night to make up for. Work can wait.'

* * *

Alana picked up her mobile, and saw that she had an incoming call from Jack. Her pulse kicked up a gear – she had a pretty good idea what the call would be about. She let it ring a few more times while she decided which tactic to employ before swiping to answer.

Jack's angry voice bellowed into her ear before she even had a chance to speak. 'I've got a bone to pick with you! A very *BIG* bloody bone! What the fuck were you thinking, telling Olivia that I used to hit you!'

'Because I was pissed at her for coming over here, acting all girly-girly. Like we could be BFFs, or something,' Alana defended.

'That's so cheap, Alana. Really?'

'Cheap! Well, she seemed to know an awful lot about me – about my past. Things that only you and I knew. Explain that to me, Jack! You must have told her things about me...'

Jack sighed. 'Maybe I did... Olivia was beginning to feel threatened by our friendship. I had to try and explain the depth of our bond, even though we're divorced. But what you said about me hitting you – that was just way out of line. I think you owe us both an apology. Olivia's devastated that you could lie like that. We trusted you. We trusted that you – as my ex-wife – would be adult enough to stay without animosity. It was no more than a business arrangement, for fuck's sake. We could have said no to your booking...'

'Look, I'm sorry! Okay! It was wrong of me. I shouldn't have said those things. But my mouth engaged before my brain, and before I knew it...'

'Yes, before you knew it, you spewed forth a load of bullshit!' His voice increased with his anger. 'Alana, I nursed you through thick and thin. How could you do this to me? How could you lie about our marriage?'

Alana could hear the sound of him banging his fist onto his desk, which made her jump in auto-response. Her mind raced, fishing for words.

'I'm really sorry, Jack. I don't know what's going on in my head, what with everything that's been happening here recently.' She took a deep breath and allowed tears to spill over, her defensive resolve having crumbled. 'I'm going to take the day off tomorrow, and go and visit some old friends. A change of scenery will be good for me. Good to get away from here...' Though upset, Alana still managed to skirt the truth about who she was going to visit.

Satisfied that his ex was genuinely remorseful, Jack softened a little. 'Fine, that sounds like a good idea... But, please, Alana – no more bullshit. Otherwise you'll find your booking cut short. Is that understood?'

Alana nodded as she answered. 'Understood. And please convey my sincere apologies to Olivia. I didn't mean to upset her or frighten her. Or upset you, Jack. Again, I'm sorry to both of you...'

She disconnected the call, and banged her head on the table. It was preferable to the pain that was shooting around in the back of her head and shoulders.

Chapter 23

Spires and Scabs

Thursday 13th August, 2015

"It's shite weather today, so I'm not going anywhere. Going to stay here in the barn. I've got the cats for entertainment, and I've got some scavenged packs of sausage rolls from the supermarket bins. Plus, I've got a couple of books to read. I've re-read them a thousand times, but they're worth it. They're good. They're Alana's books. It seems strange referring to her as Alana when I've only ever known her as Elaine. Today I will just have to read her instead of watching her...

I got the books purely by chance. I sometimes spend the day wandering the periphery of Buxton, keeping out of the way of the main areas. But as the day wears to a close for the shops, it's safer to venture in. This is when the kindness of the shopkeepers helps to keep me alive – they give me unsold bread or sandwiches. Sometimes soup and coffee. The library was getting rid of some of their older titles and shabby books, so had a little table out front. All books, 50p each. I love books and reading – they take me to a better place. And there were two paperbacks on the table that I just had to have. Two of Alana's first novels. They were really shabby – a sign that they'd been out on loan many times, I suppose. But then again, Alana is a local author with a local following. As I handed the librarian my pound coin, she simply clasped it back in my hand and told me to take the books. To use the pound to get something to eat. Kindness.

One of the novels is set in Chesterfield. Have you ever been there? It's an old market town in Derbyshire with a famous church – The Parish Church of St Mary and All Saints. But to the locals, it's simply known as the "Crooked Spire". There are many folklore tales about why it's so crooked. One is that a virgin got married in the church, so it twisted its head to take a look; the spire will only untwist when another virgin marries there. Another folktale is that a blacksmith in Castle Ridge was persuaded by a powerful magician to shoe the hooves of the devil. The blacksmith drove a nail deep into the devil's foot, causing him to fly off in a rage. As he passed over the spire, he kicked out, and twisted it! In reality, it's probably twisted because the spire was built with unseasoned oak, and unskilled labour. Plus the weight of the lead roof. Or, at least, that's what many of the theories deduce. Anyway, I'm digressing...

The Crooked Spire features in the novel. It's her first book, The Crooked Brotherhood. It drew me straight in from the first page! The story opens with the dead body of a local politician lying in a crucifix position in the covered, arched vestibule of the church. As the story unfolds, the vicar of a nearby church is also found dead on his doorstep, as are a few other notable Derbyshire locals: a wealthy landowner, a high-ranking councillor, and a justice of the peace. The police investigation uncovers a web of intrigue and deceit connected to these people, based on their past deeds within the church. They were not as honest as they had led people to believe. And so, of course, they had to pay the ultimate price for what they'd done. I'm not going to say any more, as I don't want to spoil things for you.

The other book of Alana's which I have, is set in my old hometown of Castle Ridge. It's her second novel, called Scab!, set during the 1984-85 miners' strike. There used to be a colliery in Castle Ridge before it was forced to close, and most of the men were on strike. I remember it being a tense time, even though I was only about twelve or thirteen years old. The great divide in the community came because of the two unions – the NCB were on strike, while the UDM continued to work. Those who worked were known as "scabs". You could often hear the shouts of the picket line men when the scab-bus crossed through the picket line... "Scab! Scab! Scab!" they would chant. Alana describes everything so well in the book – all the streets, the tension, and life generally in Castle Ridge. It really took me back to my youth. Anyway, as the strike progresses, some of the working miners find their homes coming under attack – paint daubed on their house walls, a dead cat on the doorstep (this is not where I got the idea from!), pig's blood tipped over cars. That kind of thing. Then someone tampers with the brakes on the scab-bus, causing a big accident. Striking miners come under suspicion. Who is behind all this? Is it more than one person? Why? Who would have this kind of grudge? Slowly the story unfolds to reveal the who and the why.

But I'm not going to tell you..."

Chapter 24

Turning Back the Clock

Friday 14th August, 2015

The train slowed as it approached Chesterfield Station, creating a Mexican wave of passengers' hands as they reached for their bags or folded up their newspapers. Alana had received a Messenger message from Will earlier in the week saying that he would be going over to Castle Ridge this coming Friday to sort out some family business, and wondered if she would like to meet up and go to the cemetery together. After figuring out the transport details, Alana caught the 9:58 from Buxton, arriving in Chesterfield at 11:54. Will had agreed to pick her up from the station in his car. She checked her reflection in the little compact hand mirror, and added a slick of natural pink lip gloss. Her pulse began to increase along with the butterflies in her stomach as she tried to imagine what Will would look like. It felt almost like going on some kind of blind date, except this would be a different kind of strangers' meeting.

Without doubt, the past would be raked up, talked about and mulled over. Yet it might hopefully bring some kind of closure, both for her and for Will's family. Maybe ghosts from the past could finally be laid to rest. So for the rest of today, she would be Elaine McCairn, not Alana McQueen.

She recalled that they were a dark-haired family, and that Will had just turned thirty, so she used this as her yard-stick for searching him out on the platform. Then again, he would probably be the one to spot her first, if he had seen her author-profile, and pictures on her website. Alana picked up her handbag, and stood to join the other alighting passengers as the train pulled to a stop.

A young man holding a single white rose cautiously stepped forward, his dark eyes glossy with welled-up tears. His eyes connected with hers, causing her own to fill up. Will held out his hand ready to shake hers – a gesture of polite first-contact, followed by a coy smile.

She was now Elaine McCairn from Castle Ridge.

Knowing that she would be uncomfortable with sitting in the front seat, Elaine had asked if it would be okay to sit in the back. This, of course, was no problem for Will. He was happy to comply with whatever made Elaine feel relaxed.

As they drove along the A632 towards Castle Ridge, Elaine could feel the years peeling away, taking her back to her youth. There was something about Will's personality and tone of voice that helped to put her at ease. After their initial meeting at the station, they had hugged each other close, and cried without abandon, oblivious to the throng of passengers going about their business. Years of pent-up emotion had been released without a single word needing to be said; a moment that bonded them, each understanding the other's pain. And now here he was, chatting and relaxed.

'...And there's the hospital on the left,' said Will, having now taken on the role of tour guide as well as chauffeur. 'The old motorbike showroom has long-since gone, though...'

Elaine watched as they passed by familiar old landmarks, now blended with much that she didn't recognise. The green fields of her youth were housing estates. Pubs were boarded up. Time had changed so much. Will's voice cut into her daydreams.

'The pits have all closed, of course. They're now memorials to the industry. And the old coking plant at the bottom of the valley has gone. Remember the smell?' Will looked in the rear-view mirror to make sure that he still had Elaine's attention.

She smiled at his reflection. 'Oh, yes, I remember that smell – it clung to everything. I'm sure the locals prefer the cleaner air!' Her stomach lurched a little, knowing that they would soon be rounding the bend towards Castle Ridge.

And there it was, perched in all its glory – the castle standing proud and ever-watchful over the valley. It was one of those visions that, no matter how long you had been away, always put a moment of pride into your heart. Castle Ridge Castle was an iconic ancient monument, and one that the locals were rightly proud and protective of.

Will noticed her looking up towards the escarpment. 'Maybe we could visit the castle later, if you like? I haven't been for years. I hear that they've done loads to it.'

Elaine nodded and shrugged. 'Sure, sounds good.'

As they drove up Colliery Hill, Will pointed out the estate on the left. 'That's where me dad's from. He was an estate lad. Whereabouts did you live, Elaine?'

A knot formed in her stomach as she recalled her childhood home. It was nothing more than squalor. 'I used to live in a small row of terraces not too far from the hosiery factory.'

'Really! My gran – Nanna Beryl – and my Aunty Brenda used to work at the factory until we moved to Skeggie. It was demolished a few years ago – it's now a housing estate.'

Will's car wound its way through the town centre of Castle Ridge. Elaine noticed that the Co-op was no longer there. In fact, many of the shops had vanished, or changed hands. She barely recognised the place. Nor did she recognise any faces. Even though she had visited the cemetery year after year, she had always directed the taxi driver to go the "back way" as she called it, thus avoiding the main shopping area. On the one hand, she felt a strange kind of relief in seeing that Castle Ridge had moved on. Yet on the other, she felt strangely disappointed, having expected to see it stuck in some kind of time-warp.

They turned the corner to head in the direction of the cemetery. Sadly, many of the cornfields that she remembered as a kid were now covered in concrete and houses.

Will pointed to an area of well-tended gardens. 'That's where me dad had his allotment. He was well proud of his veg,' he laughed. 'The locals fought hard with the town Council to keep the allotments, and not turn them into building land.'

Elaine noticed that the large field opposite was still green. 'What about the Lodge Field – do they still have the annual Castle Ridge Feast on there?'

Will shook his head. 'Nah, the Feast hasn't been here for years. A sign of the times, I suppose. Most kids prefer computer games these days. I used to love going when I was little. The nearby Lodge House and Gardens have gone, too.'

'That's a shame. It was a rite of passage for every kid to go to the Feast – the progression from the kiddie rides to the fast rides. That, and winning a goldfish!'

Will laughed. 'Ah, yes! The goldfish – they only used to last for about a week afterwards. Can you remember the name of the company that brought the Feast? Was it Proctors?'

Elaine pondered for a moment. 'Hmm… I thought it was Holland's. Or maybe it was a blend of the two? I'm not sure, to be honest.'

'I'll have to ask my dad. Perhaps he remembers.'

'So, I bet you're too young to remember the Summer Fayres that were held in the Lodge Gardens? I used to climb over the wall and sneak in! It was a magical place for a kid. All those beautiful old conker trees…'

'Yep, that's a bit before my time. My dad won a little teddy bear at the Fayre, and gave it to Mum. It was his first gift to her on their first proper date!'

'Aww, that's so sweet.'

'Young love, eh. That little teddy became our Jon's first teddy. I ended up with Dad's giraffe. Mum and Dad donated them to us when we were born. Happy days.'

Elaine's stomach suddenly began to tie itself in knots as she noticed the signpost for the cemetery up ahead. She sensed a change in Will's mood, too. He had become much quieter, more solemn.

He parked the car, then waited a moment before speaking. 'We don't have to do this, not if you don't want to...'

'No, Will. This *is* something that we have to do. Together.'

Elaine took Will's arm, and they headed to the Children's Garden of Rest to Jon's plot, their steps slow and measured.

Bird sounds filled the air, punctuated by the call of a wood pigeon in a nearby tree. 'It's so peaceful here, isn't it?' commented Elaine.

'Aye. I'm sure that Jon found peace here. C'mon, let's go and sit on that bench over there.'

Once seated, Elaine couldn't help herself and broke down into tears. 'I'm so, so sorry, Will. It was an accident – you know that, right? The locals virtually tortured me and my boyfriend with their accusations. Saying that we must have been speeding, or not paying attention, or been drinking... But none of it's true. You must believe me, Will...'

Will took her hand and held it. 'I know it was an accident. It was a shock to all of us. But yes, we know that it was an accident. It was really strange for me, losing me twin brother. We might have been different in character, but we were still inseparable.'

'What do you think Jon would have been like, if he'd still been alive today?' asked Elaine.

Will laughed, and snorted. 'Crazy! He was a chancer, even as a kid. Probably something adrenaline-related, like a racing driver. Or something with boys' toys, like a digger driver.'

Elaine noticed how his eyes sparkled with brotherly love as he pondered his late-brother's future, had it existed. Quiet moments passed before either of them spoke, as if ordering their thoughts and emotions.

'What about your mum and dad?' she asked.

'Dad somehow managed to hold it together. Men had to be men, I suppose. But my mother found it hard to cope, and had a breakdown. Plus she got cheated by some fake spiritualist from what I've been told. And, well, I guess you know that she took her own life?'

Elaine hung her head, allowing her hair to cover her face and cover her shame. 'Yes, I had heard. I'm really sorry about that. I can't begin to imagine what pain your family has been through.' She paused and took a deep breath. 'Your dad must really hate me for what I did to your family. I put two people that he loved into the ground!' Her voice began to crack, wracked by years of guilt. 'How do you think that makes me feel?'

'Of course he doesn't hate you. Nor does he blame you. In fact, he still thinks it was unfair that you and your boyfriend were being made into scapegoats. My grandmother – my mother's mother – needed to have someone to blame so she apparently fuelled a lot of the ill-will towards you both.'

'But your mum took her—'

Will laid his hand on hers, stopping her in her flow of speaking. 'Mum was always a bit highly strung. Her life had to be perfect. You didn't kill her, Elaine. Mum's death was by her own hand – her own choice. Not yours. And Jon's death was an accident. You were all in the wrong place at the wrong time.'

Elaine sighed. 'Aye, you can say that again. But how did you manage to deal with everything? You were so young – it must have been so difficult to make sense of all the loss.'

Will nodded sagely. 'Yes, it was. I remember thinking that my mum must have loved Jon more than me, to do what she did. But Dad reassured me that she went to be with Jon to take care of him, knowing that I would be safe with Dad. Moving away helped, too.' He looked at Elaine, and smiled. 'And as I grew older, I found it helpful to talk to a therapist. In fact, therapy helped me so much that I chose to make it my career, and studied to become a counsellor. I wanted to help others who had been through personal trauma.'

'That's so noble of you, Will.' She patted him on the hand. 'Thanks for today. I've struggled for years to accept the past. To accept myself. I *really* think that meeting you, and coming here has helped me face my demons head-on. And to finally hear your family's side of the story.'

Will found himself slipping into counsellor-mode, and utilised his little mantra of the three-e's: empathy, encourage and empower. 'It was twenty-five years ago, Elaine. Remember, I've walked this same road as you. You have to let it go. You can't be chained and shackled with guilt forever. Look what it's done to you.' Will paused for a moment, seeing that Elaine was struggling to hold her composure. It was time to give her a change of scenery to break the mental suction of the accident. 'C'mon, I'd like to show you where Mum is buried.'

A look of horror passed through her eyes. 'I've never dared to face her...'

'Well, then maybe now's the time. Go and make your peace with her.' He took Elaine by the hand and led her through to the main part of the cemetery, where the grown-ups were laid to rest. 'It's over there, the white marble heart.'

Elaine hesitated, then looked at Will. 'Do you mind if I go alone? I'd like to speak with her in private, if that's okay with you?'

Will nodded, and let go of her hand.

Elaine approached the headstone with as much reverence as she could muster, aware that she was approaching the woman whose child she had accidentally taken the life of. The woman who had never recovered from her loss, and had taken her own life as a consequence. She stood before the heart, and silently prayed to Julie Steele, hoping that somewhere out in the cosmos Julie could hear her words of apology. Twenty-five years of pain, like a veil of darkness, slowly began to lift from Elaine's shoulders. She knew that the memories would never fade, but at least she had taken the first steps to properly healing. Of making peace with Julie. She sensed Will approaching from behind, and turned to face him.

'This must have been very difficult for you?' His gaze met Elaine's with compassion.

She nodded, her eyes loaded with unshed tears.

He held out his hand, which triggered the release of Elaine's emotions. She allowed herself a few minutes of uncontrollable sobbing before taking a few deep breaths to recompose her demeanour and wipe her eyes.

Elaine forced a smile. 'Sorry, this is turning into quite the day for crying...' She dug into her coat pocket for more tissues.

'No worries. C'mon, I'll take you to meet Grandad Jud, he's here, too. Now, there was a character!'

She took Will's arm and allowed herself to be led. Her mind was still full of unanswered questions.

'So how come your family are all living in Skegness now?' she asked, as they strolled together.

Will sighed. 'After Mum died, Dad couldn't bring himself to stay at the cottage. There were just too many memories. My other grandparents – Dad's parents – had already retired to Skeggie after having a sizeable win on the football coupons, so we just sold up, and went to live out there, too. The clean sea air did us all the world of good, although Grandad Jud ended up with lung cancer. I suppose all those years of working in the pit didn't help. And smoking. He died about five years ago. Nanna Beryl is still alive, though she seems to be developing dementia.'

'I'm sorry to hear all that. Did your dad ever remarry?'

'Nah. Mum was his one and only love. His Lady Juliet, as he used to call her. From Romeo and Juliet. That was one of their favourite Shakespeare plays.' Will laughed. 'One of the reasons that my name is William.' It was the lighter moment that they both needed to break their solemn mood. 'Talking of names, how or why did you choose your pen-name, Alana McQueen?'

'I guess it's just a fancy version of my birth name. Alana sounds rather grand, and McQueen sounds regal. Much more "author-sounding" than Elaine McCairn, don't you think? I hoped that it would help to bury my past.'

'And did it?' Will looked at her, his eyes full of compassion for this broken woman standing beside him.

Elaine gave a weak smile in return. 'Only sometimes…'.

Will's stomach rumbled, making him chuckle. 'Well, I don't know about you, but I'm getting hungry. Shall we head up to the Castle and get something to eat in the coffee shop? And then I'll treat us to tickets to have a look around. How does that sound?'

Elaine had to concede that she felt mentally drained and exhausted, and was ready to get out of the cemetery.

'That sounds like a great idea, Will. Thanks, yes, let's do that.' She paused before continuing. 'And once again, thanks for today. This must have taken an awful lot of courage for you to find me and get in touch. And it was certainly the right thing for us to do. I think we both needed to make this visit together.' She closed her eyes, and took a deep breath; her voice on the verge of breaking. 'I am so very, very sorry for all of this…'.

'And it must have taken you an awful lot of courage for you to come here every year and put a rose on our Jon's grave… I hope that today will give us both some much needed closure.'

Elaine gave a wan smile. 'Yes, I hope so, too.'

Chapter 25

Ghosts of Decades Past

Friday 14th August, 2015

The cottage seemed eerily devoid of all sounds – not even the hum of the refrigerator, or the ticking of the kitchen clock permeated the dense silence. Alana could feel a strange stabbing sensation fleeting through her mind, as though the neurons were sparking with a lightning-strength ferocity. Had it been a good idea to meet Will today, and go with him to the cemetery? Absently, she flicked the switch on the kettle to make herself a cup of tea.

For all the years that she had been visiting Jon's grave to place the white rose, she had never dared venture beyond the Children's Garden of Rest to find Julie's grave – Jon's mother. The guilt of playing a part in Jon's premature demise weighed heavily enough, without feeling a part of his mother's. A mother who, by her own hand, had died of a broken heart. Yet today Alana had felt the need to face this element of her past. She had found the courage to speak to Julie.

The atmosphere in the kitchen took on a charged feel, making the strange sensation in Alana's head feel even stronger, the tightness painful. She swayed slightly, grabbing the edge of the sink to steady herself, not daring to pick up the now-boiling kettle.

"So, you think that stopping by my grave today absolves you of any guilt, or wrong-doing, do you?"

Alana froze, her breathing now coming in short jags. Was the voice in her head, or...? The throbbing in her temples pounded in time with her pulse.

"Turn around, and see what you've done to us..."

Surely the voice must be in her head? Yet it sounded so close, so real. She closed her eyes and turned around, only opening them once she knew she was facing the direction of the voice. She opened her eyes, allowing them to refocus. Before her, sat at the kitchen table with Jon on her knee, was Julie. Not solid, yet not translucent. Like the projected image from an old cine-camera; surreal, in sepia and white.

'Are you a ghost?'

Julie laughed, causing her image to shake and blur around the edges. *"A ghost? Do you believe in ghosts, Elaine?"*

'I... I'm not sure...'

"No, I'm not a ghost. I'm your guilty conscience. I'm here because you brought me here."

'No! I came to you today to make my peace with you!' Alana's voice cracked as she tried to explain.

"Make peace with me! Look what you did to me and my son! Can you imagine what it's like, being in a cold, dark hole in the ground? Can you imagine what it's like having worms crawl through your hair? Well, can you?!" Julie's voice sounded hollow and distorted. The mind-formed spectre continued her tirade. *"Am I scaring you, Elaine? Think yourself lucky that I'm presenting the clean image! What if I were to present the real image – the rotten, fetid, decomposed image? How would you like that, you worthless piece of shit!"*

'It was an accident – you have to believe me! I would never do anything to harm anyone, especially not a child...' Tears began overflowing, stinging her cheeks with their saltiness, while mucus ran down the back of her throat and down her nose, causing her to gag.

"And now you've met my other son, William, and charmed him with your apologies. Do you see this child sitting here on my knee? He should have had the same chances as Will to grow up! I will never forgive you for taking our lives!"

'Stop! Please, stop! I have re-lived and replayed that moment in my mind EVERY-SINGLE-DAY for the past twenty-five years...' Her sobbing made it difficult to catch her breath and speak. 'I – can't – do – it – any more... I can't do this... please... PLEASE...'

But Julie hadn't finished raping Alana's subconscious mind and probed ever deeper, enveloping her rationale with dark shadows. *"Did you really think that running away and reinventing yourself would absolve you, Elaine McCairn? Pretending to be someone new! Did you really think that you deserved to escape your guilt? Well! Did you?"*

Alana sank to the floor, and buried her face to her knees, wrapping her hands over her head and ears to block out the voice and vision of Julie and Jon. Her mind felt cold and numb. 'Leave me alone...' she whispered. 'Please, Julie... Leave me alone. I have to find peace...'

Julie's papery-thin voice cut deep into Alana's mind. *"There is only one true way to find peace, Elaine..."*

Chapter 26

You Have 1 New Message...

Saturday 15th August, 2015

Exhausted, Alana set some milk to warm in the microwave. A soothing, creamy mug of hot chocolate was in order. The spectral images of last night's visitation from Julie and Jon had continued to torture Alana's mind throughout the day, making deep concentration and writing focus virtually impossible. As much as she tried not to believe in ghosts, there were occasions when this belief was challenged. And Julie's scathing accusations were so unfair. After all, ghosts tended to stick around the place where they died, or had spent the most time when alive. Didn't they? Her temples pulsed as she battled with her thoughts. Surely it must have been in her mind? But if nothing else, the horrors of the mind-images had helped Alana to add some graphic embellishment to her latest work in progress. It was the only positive outcome to a shitty day.

Her daydreams were interrupted by the *ping* of the microwave. Yet in her distracted state of mind, the *ping* belonged to her phone. She picked it up.

With her subconscious now disassociated from reality, the phone screen showed that she had one new message. Alana pressed the blue icon. It was from a private number. Alana sighed; she could never understand why people couldn't be upfront and open about who they are. What did they have to hide? But then again, wasn't she herself ex-directory, cut off from the mainstream of public life, and hiding behind pen-name anonymity?

She "opened" the imagined message.

"Hi Alana! How are you today? I thought I'd better check in with you!"

Although irritated by the fact she had no clue who the message was from, Alana deigned to be polite, and typed out a courteous reply. "I'm fine, thanks. And you?"

"Not too bad, despite feeling cold and damp."

She tapped the screen of her phone with her nails, puzzled by the cryptic reply. "That's good…" Alana quickly added another message to follow. "Sorry, who is this, by the way?"

"It's me. And it's you…"

"That doesn't make any sense!!!" she replied.

"Who do you think it is?"

"I don't know. That's why I'm asking!'

"Who do you want it to be?"

"Is it you, Will?"

"No. But it's someone who's very close to Will."

Alana began grinding her teeth. Of course it wasn't Will – he would have called her Elaine, not Alana… Besides which, he didn't have her private phone number. "Look, I really don't have time for this BS! Who is this?"

"I told you – someone very close to Will. And Jon. And Julie. And VERY close to you…"

A knot formed in Alana's stomach as she typed her reply. "What do you mean by that? WHO ARE YOU?"

"I am all the dark shadows of your past. And I am all the dark shadows of your mind."

The hairs on Alana's forearms rose involuntarily with goosebumps, and the back of her neck bristled. "Stop playing games, this isn't funny!!!"

Her phone *pinged* with the next message. *"If you had eyes inside your head, you would see me now. I'm watching over you. I'm your every move. I'm crawling inside your mind – I'm ALL your darkest thoughts."*

Alana could feel the sting of vomit in the back of her throat, and her heartbeat kicked up a gear.

Another message came before she had time to formulate a reply.

"Did you like my advice, by the way?"

"What advice?" Alana wondered why she was continuing to engage in this anonymous exchange.

"How to get rid of all your ghosts. How to truly find peace."

There was a momentary pause, then another message came.

"There's only one way out of this, Alana. Or are you Elaine? Only one way to truly find peace. Take my advice, you worthless piece of shit..."

A surge of adrenaline pushed the vomit into Alana's mouth, causing her to reach for her nearby hoodie as a catch-cloth. She retched, expelling the remains of her chicken-noodle salad, while uncontrollable tears ran down her face.

Alana's mind imploded with racing thoughts, one thought jumbling on top of the next. She threw her phone across the room, throwing away the non-existent phone-message conversation; a conversation that she had had with all the guilty demons in her mind. She crumpled down onto the floor, sobbing.

Please go away... Please leave me alone... I can't take much more of this...

Mind's Eye

Breakdown

"And then the wonderful bubble that I had created around my mind burst…

I suppose it had to at some point. I had buried my old-self in my writing, my marriage, and a name-change. I thought that if I suppressed the old me, then my old life would leave me alone.

Yes, I know what you're thinking – so why do I torture myself by going back to the grave every year when I've erased every other aspect of that life?

Penance?

Guilt?

Duty?

No – it's because I still care. This is one part of my past that I can't erase. An accident which took the lives of two people, if you count the fact that their mother committed suicide through heart-break. A family tragedy of which I am part.

But we all know what happens when you put a sticking plaster over an untreated wound – it festers under the surface until all the putrid, gangrenous rot bursts out.

And that's what happened to me.

My mind exploded.

Neither myself nor Jack realised what was happening at first. I'd been ill in bed with the flu, the winter was dark and filthy, and getting out of bed didn't feel like an option. The longer I left it, the harder it became. Jack tried to encourage me out of bed, but I either faked sleep, or lost my temper and raged at him to leave me alone. And when you're alone with the curtains drawn, the mind begins a festering descent into a dark place. It becomes a maze – a dark labyrinth full of dead ends with no way out of the chaos. It's so easy to become lost in the darkness. Fiction becomes fact. Demons and voices become real. And reality becomes the enemy. This was my first cycle of depression.

Kudos to Jack – he never gave up on me. As spring and the brighter days returned, little by little he would open the curtains a centimetre wider. Little by little, some sunshine returned to clear away the dark shadows lurking in my mind. He had the foresight to leave a notebook and pen close by, so I began exorcising my mental demons by writing things down. Some of these dark dreams later became incorporated into my work; an element of realism woven into fiction. It was strangely cleansing. It helped me to find my way out of the shadows of depression and into the light of healing.

Even though I managed to lift myself out of this dark phase and return to some semblance of daily life, I still carried a strange kind of weight on my psyche. I had been fooled by the light. There was always something lurking; something bubbling under the surface just waiting to reappear. I buckled under the pressure of trying to be "normal", of trying to be all things to all people. The grey cloud descended once again, enveloping all that I had worked so hard to push away.

And once again, Jack took care of me. Except this time he made sure that he – we – had the support of mental health specialists. Tablets and therapy became my new best friends. For a while, at least...

But you know what it's like – you think that once the tablets have "healed" the problem, that you don't need to take them any more. Wrong.

This time, I had a total breakdown.

Not only of my mind, but also my marriage.

I had buried so much, I had faked so much, that I could no longer separate reality from all that I had invented in my head. The dark shadows in my mind became a deep pit that I couldn't crawl out of. I didn't know who I was anymore.

And the voices... In my dreams I could hear the little boy's mother screaming at me. Screaming at me for taking away the life of her child. Screaming at me for taking away her life. I could hear the tortured soul of the little boy, lost in some kind of purgatory. I could hear the drunken screams of my parents as they fought.

And I could hear my own screams. Mostly at Jack, poor bloke. He had walked over hot coals to take care of me. A true knight in shining armour, if ever there was one. He deserved better than what I was putting him through. And so I pushed for a divorce. He resisted at first, but in the end he knew that it was the only option. I needed to pare my life down to absolute basics and start again. I just couldn't take any more.

That was about five years ago. Our divorce settlement gave me enough cash to get a little place of my own; a canal-side apartment in Manchester. Something completely different – a place to be anonymous without feeling lonely. Step by very slow step, I rebuilt my life to some kind of simple normality.

I was able to start writing again, and I made sure that I took better care of myself. I even had the support of a therapist to help get me through those early days of transition.

Yet here I am, back in my old cottage, in contact with my ex, and in contact with the past; with the young man whose brother I inadvertently killed.

There never really is any escape from who you really are, is there?"

Chapter 27

A Slave to the Shadows

Sunday 16th August, 2015

Alana fumbled on the bedside table for her phone; the digital numbers telling her that it was 02:43. She let it slip from her fingers and clatter back down onto the pine surface. Sleep was once again being a teasingly elusive mistress rather than a comforting bosom. She could feel the pulse of blood starting to pound in her temples; her mind felt like there was a mouse gnawing away at the dark recesses. Or was it an actual mouse that she could hear? The cottage had suffered with them in the past, especially during winter when the field mice came in from the cold. Alana absently recalled the countless traps that she'd emptied, particularly in the kitchen. The mouse in her head began laughing at her, the internal noise all consuming. Revenge for his fallen brethren.

Knowing the sleep-fight was lost, she levered herself up and plumped the pillow behind her shoulders while deciding what to do next. Night sounds became amplified in the dark; she could hear a pair of owls calling to each other, their calls haunting and melancholy. And there was definitely the scratching-scraping of a real mouse somewhere in the cavity wall. She rolled her eyes and sighed. At least it was no longer her problem.

Rather than waste any more time playing the "chase the sleep" game, Alana turned on the little bedside lamp. She blinked hard and shielded her eyes with the back of her hand while they adjusted to the intrusion of artificial light. She reached for her little goody-bag – an old make-up bag containing an assortment of left-over sleep solutions that she had amassed over the years; Melatonin, Diazepam, Nytol, sedative antihistamine... It was all in there. A veritable treasure trove for the insomniac. Alana had already taken one melatonin before bed, but the effects had been short-lived. Maybe she should have a little game of lucky-dip? Just close her eyes and see what came out?

The mouse scratched again, though she was uncertain whether it was a real mouse, or the mind-mouse.

Or...was it something outside? Was someone throwing pebbles at the windows? Maybe that's what the noise was?

Although the cottage now had the benefit of security cameras, the downside was that they came with a viewer-app. All Alana (or Jack) had to do was click on the app and she could check to see what the cameras were picking up. She stared at her phone, willing herself to make a decision.

Should she take a look?

Or not?

Her heart pumped hard while she swung between her viewing dilemmas.

Should she take a look?

Or not?

Did she really want to see someone prowling around outside?

Should she take a look?

Or not?

Alana took a deep breath – taking a look won.

She opened the app and checked both cameras. Though the external lighting only illuminated the immediate vicinity of the back patio, and front door area, nothing looked out of the ordinary. She tried to look beyond, but the crescent glow of the new moon barely lit the night sky, let alone the landscape.

A sigh of relief escaped.

Now feeling a little calmer, she made her choice of medication and grabbed the pack of Nytol. That and a milky cup of hot chocolate should at least go part way to defeating tonight's bout of irrational fear and insomnia. She grabbed her cosy robe and slippers, before heading down to the kitchen.

While she waited for the little jug of milk to warm in the microwave, Alana busied herself with mixing some hot chocolate powder and water to make a creamy paste. She loved the way that it made the drink extra frothy when the warm milk was added. It was a child-like yet comforting thing to do.

The invasive sound of the mind-mouse returned, catching her unawares. Mercifully, the hum of the microwave drowned out some of the noise in Alana's head, giving her a momentary respite from the internal mind-torture. But only for a moment. It began again as soon as the microwave *pinged* to announce its time was up.

Gnaw, gnaw, gnaw...

Gnaw, gnaw, gnaw...

Leave me alone!

GNAW, GNAW, GNAW...

GNAW, GNAW, GNAW.

Leave–me–alone!

Alana could hear the blood rushing and pounding in her head; the tightness becoming unbearable. Decision-making became a gargantuan challenge – should she take the tablet and drinking-chocolate upstairs, or sit here in the chill of the kitchen listening to all the night sounds?

It was warm upstairs.

It was cold downstairs.

It was safe upstairs.

It was unsafe downstairs.

What if it wasn't a mouse scratching?

What if...?

C'mon, Alana – you've checked the cameras. There's no-one there.

She quickly swallowed her tablet with a mouthful of drinking chocolate. Should she take another one?

No. No, that wouldn't be wise...

Stop this, Alana – you're a grown woman! This is a house that you know!

Her mind went into defensive overdrive, giving her all the reasons that she needed to feel safe.

Breathe, Alana.

There are no such things as monsters, or ghosts, or...

Just breathe.

The doors are locked and bolted...

Just breathe.

There's no-one out there...

Breath by steady breath, Alana composed herself enough to stop shaking, and make it upstairs without spilling her drink.

She snuggled herself back into bed, choosing to keep the little lamp switched on. It helped to push the dark shadows away.

Please, no more mind-games for tonight.

Please...

Chapter 28

Decision Time

Monday 17th August, 2015

Alana sat at the kitchen table and cradled her mug of tea, oblivious to the heat burning into the palms of her hands and fingers. It was already 9:30 and she had barely gotten started with her day, let alone been for a morning run. Her body ached from the restless night, her mind felt like it was stuffed full of cotton wool, and her eyes burned with tiredness. A sense of impending doom hung around her psyche like a cloak made out of lead.

She couldn't go on. Enough was enough.

Without any warning, Alana burst into tears, releasing an accumulation of frustration, fear, tiredness and self-pity. This was no longer her place, or her life. She had done all that she had come here for. It was time to tie up loose ends and...

She reached for her phone. 'Hi, Jack.'

'Hey, good morning. What's up?'

Alana snuffled, and wiped her eyes and nose with the sleeve of her sleep-shirt . 'Oh, just a shit night's sleep. Guess I'm not feeling too good. I just wanted to let you know that I'm going to cut short my stay, if that's okay. I've paid for the full month's booking, so you won't lose out. I know there's a no-refund policy.'

Jack was caught off guard. 'Well... erm, okay, if you're sure...' An unconscious feeling of relief swept through him. As much as he still cared for his ex-wife, he knew that life would be able to return to some semblance of normality once she had gone.

'I'm sure. What with everything that's happened while I've been here, I think I've outstayed my welcome. It's time for me to move on.' She laughed, trying to cover her grey mood. And, of course, she hadn't told Jack every last detail of her ghostly mind-visitations, or clandestine exchanges with Will Steele. 'I'm going to check the train times, but will most likely leave this coming Friday 21st, one week earlier than planned. I just need to wrap up a few things with my writing, and a few bits and bobs in town.'

'Okay. Keep me posted on the details – I'd like to come and see you before you leave. In fact, I'll take you to the station.'

The tension suddenly went from Alana's neck and shoulder muscles. It was the right decision. 'That's really kind of you, Jack. Thanks.' A sigh escaped. 'Ciao for now, bambino.'

Jack laughed at her use of their old telephone farewell. 'Yep, ciao for now, bambina.'

Chapter 29

A Friend in Need...

Tuesday 18th August, 2015

Ged watched, fascinated, as Will's thumbs danced across the screen of his phone. The way that the younger generations communicated – with their thumbs and a *ding*! Like Pavlov's dogs! And not even proper sentencing, or spelling. Just a series of shorthand and little emojis, or whatever they're called.

'Who are you chatting with?' Ged laughed at his selection of wording. 'Back in my day, we chatted voice to voice...'

Will looked up from his phone. 'Yeah, yeah... Back in your day, life was all rainbows and rock music, and stinky phone boxes.'

'Oh, yeah, stinky phone boxes... You young 'uns don't know how lucky you are, not to suffocate in a phone box. You've never lived! Anyway, you didn't answer my question...'

'So I don't have the right to a private life?' Will scowled and rolled his eyes, teasing his father. 'It's Elaine. Elaine McCairn. I, er... I met up with her the other day. We, erm, we went to the cemetery together...'

The colour rose in Ged's face, as he shot Will a narrow-eyed glance. 'You kept that quiet.'

'Because I knew *exactly* how you'd react.' Will exhaled loudly, irritated. 'I know you said the past can't be changed – to move on – but I sent Elaine some flowers to acknowledge her still caring about Jon. I got in touch with her, and we arranged to go to the cemetery together. Try to give things closure. She just wanted to get our perspective on things, not the Castle Ridge bias.'

Ged's reply came out curt and sharp. 'And did it give her closure?'

Will sighed. 'No, I think it made things worse... That's why Elaine was just messaging me – she seems to be having delusions. She said that Mum and Jon's ghosts came to visit her. She was terrified. Mum told her that there's only one way out of all this...'

His phone *pinged* again as another message came in from Elaine. Will looked at the message, then quickly typed a reply.

'Oh, for fuck's sake!' Ged slammed the pages of his newspaper together, then folded it with a huff.

Will inadvertently added more fuel to the now simmering fire in Ged's mood. 'She's worried that she's on the edge of another breakdown.'

'"*Another*" breakdown? You mean she's had breakdowns in the past?'

A surge of guilt cursed through Will's veins for having opened the Pandora's Box of his family's past. He nodded. 'Sorry, Dad – I didn't know it would turn out like this. I... I–'

Ged cut him off, and shot him a disapproving glance. 'Well, let's hope that she doesn't follow your mother's advice.' Ged did air-quotes with his fingers as he said "advice". 'Let's hope that she gets some help.'

It wasn't often that they had disagreements, but this one cut Will to the bone. 'That's exactly what I told her. To speak to someone – to get professional help, if that's how bad she's feeling. She's cutting short her stay at the cottage and heading home to Manchester on Friday, so maybe that will help to lay all the Castle Ridge ghosts to rest.'

'Aye, maybe. Let's hope so, for all our sakes. I don't think any of us wants to carry the burden of more tragedy...'

Will stood up and stretched. 'Anyway, I've got a bit of research work to do on the computer, then make a video-call to one of my mates.' He teasingly pulled on his dad's ponytail as he walked past him towards the office. 'Catch you later.'

'Ouch! Aye, catch y'later.' Ged checked his watch. 'I think I'll just take a stroll up to the pub for an hour or so. Don't wait up, I've got a key.'

A silent sense of relief coursed through Will. He hadn't exactly been honest with his father about who he was going to have a video-call with. Yes, it was a friend – but that friend was Elaine McCairn.

'Hi, Elaine. Nice to see you again.' Will's voice sounded hollow in the office, as he spoke towards the computer. Elaine's facial image moved sporadically on his screen, slightly out of sync with her voice. He could see from the background that she was seated in a comfy looking wing-back armchair. Her eyes looked shadowed and dull in the low-light glow of the wall-lamps.

'Hey, Will. Thanks for agreeing to have a video-chat with me. I'm okay with messaging, but sometimes it can get a bit tedious!' She wiggled her thumbs to him, trying to keep her mood lighter than she actually felt.

'No problem.' He took note of the beautiful painting of barn owls behind her. 'Wow! Is that a Pollyanna Pickering in the background?'

'It is! Yes. She's my favourite wildlife artist. I used to love going to her place near Matlock and browsing. I could literally have spent a fortune there! I left this owl-print here at the cottage, but I have two other Pollyanna prints back at my place in Manchester.'

'Lucky you! I usually buy one of her calendars. That's as close as I get to affording her work.' He laughed, and took note that Elaine's demeanour now looked a little more relaxed. Talking about the painting was just the ice-breaker that he'd needed. 'Anyway, I'll be straight with you – I can't offer you any counselling, as you're not my client. But we can at least chat. A problem shared is a problem halved. Isn't that how the old saying goes?'

'Something like that...' Elaine smiled at him. There was something about Will's personality that made her feel comfortable. Something that made her feel like she could offload all that was bothering her, and he would understand. She sighed before continuing. 'It's like I don't know who I am anymore. I created this new persona years ago – Alana the writer, and she became my daily *me*.' She air-quoted "me". 'But now Elaine has resurfaced and started over-riding my thoughts. It's like the safety-net of Alana has been stripped away, particularly since this visit to Derbyshire. Maybe I should have just accepted who I was, and lived my life as that person, rather than try and live as someone else. Maybe I should have gotten counselling as Elaine, not Alana.'

Will watched and listened intently. He could see tears building in her eyes. 'We can all wear some kind of mask, Elaine. We can all consciously act differently, talk differently, depending who we're with. Our private life is usually very different from our public persona.'

'Yes, I understand that. But it's like I can no longer differentiate between the reality that I'm living, or the fiction that I'm writing. I don't know what's real anymore. I don't know *who I am*, anymore...'

Will sat back in his chair, and pondered a moment. 'I don't know if you've ever heard of the psychiatrist, Carl Jung, but he described the human psyche as having a dark shadow – the negative or primitive side to one's personality. Ordinarily, we keep this side suppressed because we live by morals and social norms. But occasionally, this side of us can slip out – like with a slip-of-the-tongue, for example. Everyone carries a shadow, Elaine. For some, to a lesser degree; for others, the shadow is darker.' Realising that their conversation was slipping towards a therapy session, Will changed tactics, and tried his best to sound more "chummy". 'The burdens of our past can weigh heavy, Elaine. Some people find it difficult to offload their burden. I think of it in terms of the "sticking plaster" analogy – putting a plaster over a wound that hasn't been properly cleaned is asking for trouble. Over time, the wound will fester beneath, until eventually all the infection, all the rot and badness, bursts out.'

She nodded her understanding. 'That's true. So, what you're saying is, if you create some kind of artificial persona, then sooner or later the deeply rooted dark shadow will burst forth? Alana became my sticking plaster, covering over the wounds of Elaine. Perhaps I should go back to being Elaine as my ordinary, everyday persona, and just use Alana McQueen as a pen-name for my books? Keep the two entities very separate. Fancy that – Alana was really the bad guy! The antagonist!' She laughed and shook her head at the author-analogy that she'd just made. 'All that happened in Castle Ridge – my life back then, the accident – none of it was my fault. You're right, Will. I have to stop blaming myself. I have to stop blaming Elaine for all that has gone wrong in my life...' She closed her eyes and took a deep breath, as though she had just had her epiphany.

Seeing her demeanour change from uptight to softer and calmer gave Will a feeling of accomplishment. The same feeling he often had when he saw his clients finally have their moment of acceptance, or start to see their world in a more positive light.

'Exactly. You had to create your own standards. After all, you had no decent role models to learn from, if you think about it...'

The sound of the front door opening and closing suddenly made him jump. Knowing full-well that his dad wouldn't approve, he kept his voice low.

'Elaine, I'm sorry, but I have to go. My dad's back from the pub, and I would rather our conversation stayed private. This is *our* time.'

'No problem, I understand. And thanks again...'

She just had time to wave to Will before his screen disconnected with hers.

Chapter 30

Loose Change. Loose Ends.

Wednesday 18th August, 2015

Frustrated by his overwhelming desire to make contact with "his Elaine", the free-walker threw his binoculars down by his side. The heat of the day was already rising, causing the smell from his old clothes to ripen. He gagged from his own body odour. How on earth could he present himself – all that he had become, all that he now was – to Elaine? He shielded his eyes from the bright glow of the corn stubble, and blinked away the building moisture. Were they tears because the sun was stinging his eyes, or were they the tears of a heartbroken man?

He stood up and stretched, then went to take a piss behind the old drystone walling. There had to be something that he could do.

Some way of getting to speak to Elaine.

Some way of not scaring the hell out of her.

But what would he say to her?

Could he still even speak? After all, it was decades since he last had a real conversation with anyone. Chatting with the barn-cats didn't really count.

As he zipped up his trousers, the weight of coins in his pocket reminded him that he was not totally penniless. Maybe he had enough to buy some new clothes from the charity shop? The staff had often been kind enough to help him out. Perhaps if he explained his plight? He wiped the drips of piss from his fingertips onto his trousers, then fumbled in his pocket for his coins. His total fiscal worth amounted to a measly £4.87. Money that he had either found or begged. He sighed. Not much, but at least the last of his money would go to a good cause.

Suddenly hit by a wave of defeat, he fell to his knees and allowed himself the privilege of sobbing until he was exhausted.

This time he knew that the tears were those of a heartbroken man.

Tears for a lost life.

Tears for a lost love.

He awoke behind the drystone wall with the sun high above him. A fly buzzed around his head, eager to drink his escaped saltiness. Realising that he'd fallen to sleep in the patch of grass where he'd earlier taken a piss, he tried to dust off his trousers in defiant dignity, but his right arm tingled with pins and needles making even this simple task difficult. His mouth and throat felt dry. It was just too hot to be out here in the open field. He needed the cool shelter of the woodland, and a cleansing splash in the little river.

As he strode down the field towards the woods, he felt buoyed by a renewed sense of urgency. A renewed sense of hope. This could probably be his last chance of making contact with Elaine. He would get freshened up as best he could, then head into Buxton. See if he could beg for some better clothes.

Sudden movement in the back garden of the cottage registered in the periphery of his vision and caught his attention. Elaine was outside.

He changed the course of his direction...

* * *

Alana leaned back in her patio chair and crossed her legs at the ankles. She moved her sunglasses from the top of her head and put them in their rightful place on her nose. Strange how people use their sunglasses as a headband – it was something that she thought was pretentious, yet here she was doing it. She ran her fingers through her hair to muss it up. Today was living up to its forecast. Her shoulders felt heavy with the heat. Or was it her mood causing the heaviness? She scanned the garden and sighed. It was so beautiful here, that much she had to admit. The flowers and shrubs were in full bloom, and she'd even managed to get some raspberries from the old raspberry canes. A garden that she had established, nurtured and enjoyed. Yet at this moment in time, it gave her no joy. A feeling of immense emptiness swept over her. As calming as the countryside could be, it could also be a very lonely place if you were not part of the local cliques. She grabbed her phone and dialled her agent's number, then got up to stretch her legs and take a stroll around the shrubs and flower borders. It was time to start finalising her plans.

"Judith! Hi! – Yes, I'm fine, how are you? – That's great. Anyway, I just wanted to let you know that I'm heading back into Manchester on Friday. – A-ha. – Yes, I've finished everything. All done and dusted. I'll email all the stuff over to you later today. – Oh, and there's a little extra-something for you that I've been working on. – A-ha. Yes, I'll stop by your office next week..." She stopped mid-sentence and listened. Was that a twig that she just heard snapping behind the laurel and holly bushes? *"What? Yes, sorry, I'm still here, Judith. Just thought I heard something in the garden. This place is starting to creep me out... Lovely. – Okay, see you next week."*

She disconnected the call, and stood stock-still, listening to every movement in the garden. Everything sounded natural – nothing out of the ordinary. Yet she couldn't resist shouting out –

'If there's anyone there, please stop this. It's very wrong to spy on people...'

'Who are you talking to?'

Alana screamed, then swung around, ready to launch an attack at the voice behind her.

'Jack! What are you doing here? Don't creep up on people like that, for fuck's sake!' Her voice was shaky, nervous. 'Sorry... I, er, I thought there was someone in the garden. I thought I heard something...' she explained.

'It's the middle of the day, Alana. No-one is going to spy on you in broad daylight... Anyway, I brought lunch for us.' He held up a paper bag full of goodies from the local bakery. He placed the bag down on the little patio table, before coming to give her a peck on each cheek.

Alana's shoulders relaxed a little, and she exhaled loudly. 'Sorry. Thanks, Jack – that's very thoughtful of you. Just...just don't creep up on people like that. Anyway, I never heard you knock. Do you normally walk in on people without knocking?' she chided.

'I did knock. But I could hear your voice in the garden, so guessed you were on the phone.' He rummaged in the paper bag to get out the sandwiches and pastries, before sitting down.

'I was just speaking to Judith, my agent. I wanted to let her know that I'm heading back on Friday, ahead of schedule.'

Jack finished chewing his bite of sandwich, then wiped his mouth with a paper napkin. 'Ah, that's one of the reasons I'm here. Did you figure out the train times, so that I can pick you up and take you to the station? It's really no bother. And it's been lovely to see you again.' He put his hand over hers.

She gave him a wan smile in return, before gently pulling her hand away. 'Thanks, Jack. It's been a strange visit, what with one thing and another. But if I'm honest, I can't say that I've one-hundred percent enjoyed my time here. Yes, it's been very productive, work-wise. But sadly, it hasn't been good for my mental health...' Alana pushed her sunglasses back onto the top of her head, and her eyes met with Jack's. 'There have just been too many memories, and not all of them good.'

'Aye, I'm sure it's been a bit strange. But some of the bad feelings have been of your own making... Like going to the graveyard for one, and meeting with Will Steele–'

Alana sighed, and held up her hand defiantly. 'Okay, let's stop this conversation right now, Jack. I don't need you to tell me what's right and wrong.' Her mind began flipping and sparking, causing her heart-rate to increase. She closed her eyes and took a few deep breaths. 'But going back to your earlier question – yes, I've sorted out my train ticket for Friday. It's the 13:58 from Buxton to Manchester Piccadilly. And thank you – it's very kind of you to take me to the station.'

'No probs, bambina. And sorry, I didn't mean to upset you.'

'I know. I know. But back off, Jack. I've just got a few loose ends to tie up today, with the manuscript and stuff, and then–'

'And then you'll be gone.' Jack looked at his ex-wife and smiled. 'I'm really happy for you, Alana. Happy that you've made a successful career out of your writing. That you were able to show the world what a great talent you have. You really kicked life in the balls!' He raised his can of lemon-flavoured soda water as a toast.

'Amen to that, Jack.' She raised her own can and gently clinked it with his, then added an afterthought. 'Not bad for some old chick from Castle Ridge...'

He watched and listened from behind the damp depths of the laurel and holly bushes, while they sat in the sunshine, laughing, eating, chatting. A fallen holly leaf prickled his bony backside. An apt metaphor, if ever there was one. Jealousy bit deep into the pit of his stomach, sharing a place with the hunger that was gnawing there.

He imagined himself swapping places with the man at the table.

He imagined himself laughing, eating, chatting.

He imagined himself clean-shaven, and wearing nice clothes.

He imagined...

He imagined...

He imagined his heart not breaking every time he saw her.

Chapter 31

An Unexpected Visitor

Thursday 20th August, 2015

'Hi, Elaine.'

'Will – what are you doing here?'

'Sorry – I know that it's a bit late. Perhaps I should have called you first. But I was just on my way home from a seminar in Manchester, so thought I would make a detour into Buxton. I just came to say goodbye, and, erm, give you these...' Will proffered a bouquet of white roses towards her hand. 'There's twenty-five – one for each year that, well, you know... Plus I brought a book for you. It's by Carl Jung – the psychiatrist that I was telling you about. Extracts from his work. I was a bit worried about you after the texts you sent me the other day, and after our video-chat. This might help you understand some of the psychology connected to the dark shadows, and stuff. It might help you to stop feeding into it.' He looked at her, his eyes loaded with compassion.

'That's really thoughtful of you. Thank you.' She accepted the bouquet and book with a flustered gesture. 'Well, I'd hardly call eight o'clock late. I keep trying to put it all out of my mind, for the time being, at least. In fact, I was just about to crack open a box of Thornton's Continentals and make a pot of coffee. Would you like to come in, and help me celebrate? It's a bit naff celebrating a writing completion all by yourself!' She forced a laugh to cover her low mood and stepped to one side, encouraging him to come inside.

'Well, if Thornton's chocolates are on offer, how can I resist!' He went inside, and followed her through to the kitchen, noting that her bags were all packed and ready in the hallway.

'It's nice of you to make the detour. Yep, back to the big city tomorrow.' She absently began busying herself with the cafetière and kettle, before finding a vase for the roses. 'It's been a strange few weeks,' she continued. 'And none more so than using my old name, and meeting you. It certainly raked up a lot of memories...' She remained with her back to Will, before pausing at the sink.

He noticed that her shoulders were beginning to shake, and she hung her head. A loud sob escaped.

'I'm so sorry, Elaine – I didn't mean to upset you!' Will jumped up, and clumsily tried to offer her some comfort. 'Here, come and sit down, I'll make the coffee.' He guided her to sit at the table.

She shook her head. 'It's okay. It's just been really strange being back here. It was a total mistake. My whole life seems to have flashed before my eyes... The pressure of writing, seeing my ex happy with his new wife, visiting the graveyard, and stuff. And to top it off, I'm pretty sure there's some nutter of a tramp following me! There's been some weird shit happening while I've been here...' She glanced at the kitchen window, her eyes wide as if expecting to see a face. 'There's no wonder I feel like I'm on the edge of another breakdown...' She buried her face in her hands, her sobs building in intensity.

Will passed her the roll of kitchen paper so that she could wipe her face and eyes, then sat down, quietly waiting for Elaine's crying to subside. He poured two cups of coffee and opened the box of chocolates in the hope of distracting her. Dealing with crying women was something he usually encountered on a professional level, not a friendship level. Maybe his dad had been right to let sleeping dogs lie, and not get involved with raking up the past. It couldn't be changed. It wouldn't bring back his mother or Jon. He sighed.

Elaine picked up her coffee and began toying with the box of chocolates while she selected one. 'I don't know how much longer I can live with all this... Day after day, there's always something to cloud my mind. I'm no longer sure what's imagined or what's real. Voices. Images. And like I told you the other day, even your mother came to speak to me. She said some horrible things – she blamed me for everything...'

'Elaine, there are no such things as ghosts! You have to try and let go of the past.' He glanced over at the roses, regretting giving them to her. Twenty-five reminders of the past.

'She was sitting right there, I tell you. Your brother was sitting on her knee!' Tears began welling in her eyes again. 'In fact, I swear it was her that sent me an SMS message the other night. It's like she was in my head, but she was also in my phone! She said she was my conscience. She was watching over my shoulder. Here, look!' She pushed her phone towards Will, open at the Messages app.

Will took the phone and scrolled through the list of recent SMS conversations: with Jack, with her agent, with a couple of friends. But nothing from beyond the grave from his mother, and certainly nothing that looked malicious. Taken aback by the conviction and ferocity of her voice, he stared at her while trying to gather his thoughts. He drew on his professional knowledge as a counsellor. Playing it down and not feeding into it would be the only way. 'Look, there's nothing here in your phone. Nothing from my mother. No malicious messages from anyone. I'm sorry for the things you think that my mother said to you. She's clearly taken her grief and accusations to the grave with her. But *we* know that it wasn't your fault. *We* know that it was an accident. And that's what counts.' He put his hand over hers to try and reassure her, and snap her out of her self-loathing. 'There's nothing here to be afraid of. C'mon, have another chocolate – we're supposed to be celebrating the closure of your work...' He pushed the box towards her.

For a few breath-stopping moments, nothing could be heard but the sound of the kitchen clock, ticking away the seconds. Will swallowed, fearing that he'd overstepped the mark.

Elaine stared blankly, unseeing, as she spoke. 'But... I swear... I must be going nuts.'

'You're not going nuts, Elaine. You've just had a lot to deal with lately.'

She refocused, her eyes seeking Will's. 'I'm sorry – you didn't come here for this. You didn't come here to listen to some batty woman talking about ghosts...'. She sighed, and tried to compose herself with a distraction. 'Tell me about yourself, Will. Apart from being a counsellor, I don't really know anything else about you. Are you married? Do you have any kids?'

'No, and no. I was almost married, but things didn't work out. I met someone when I was at uni, and we got engaged. All was going well, but then after we graduated, she got a job offer in the States – which she accepted. I just couldn't leave Dad. So, sadly, our relationship ended. I haven't really met anyone since. Been on a few dates, but nothing serious. I've gotten used to the freedom of doing my own thing.'

'Same here. I haven't bothered with anyone else since Jack and I divorced. Relationships just complicate matters!'

'I'll drink to that,' laughed Will, and he lifted his coffee cup towards Elaine's in a gesture of "cheers". 'Anyway, I suppose I'd better get on my way. I've still got a few hours' drive to get back to Skeggie.'

'Wouldn't you be better off checking into a hotel in Buxton, and then driving home fresh in the morning? It's Friday tomorrow – surely you could make a long weekend out of your trip', suggested Elaine.

Will yawned and stretched. 'D'you know what – that sounds like a great idea. I'll take a drive down there and see what's available. Better give the old man a call too, so that he doesn't worry.' He stood up ready to leave, about to offer Elaine a handshake, only to change it into a hug and cursory peck on the cheek. 'Listen – will you promise to go and see a counsellor when you get back to Manchester? Please get some help, Elaine. I'm talking to you as a professional now, not just a friend.'

Elaine nodded, and hugged him back. 'Yes, I promise... I have a lot of self-evaluation to do.'

As they headed from the kitchen to the front door, neither were aware that their entire evening had been observed from the shadows.

And neither were aware of the French doors opening while this unexpected – and unwelcome – visitor slipped in, unseen and unheard.

Chapter 32

An Unwelcome Visitor

Thursday 20th August, 2015

After waving goodbye to Will, Elaine dropped the Yale lock on the front door, then began her rituals of locking and bolting the kitchen door and the French doors at the rear. Once satisfied that all was secure, she headed up the stairs to spend her last night at the cottage.

Her reflection stared back at her from the bathroom mirror while she brushed her teeth, and she shivered. Signs of dark rings were visible below her eyes. Too much computer work and not enough sleep. She absently mused over the past month, grateful that she'd not only completed the work for her next novel, but produced a solid first draft for another, loosely based on this retreat. All in all, it had been a productive four weeks despite the ghosts from the past, and the dark shadows invading her mind. Will had grown up into a lovely young man in spite of his losses. Yes, it was nice to have made his acquaintance. Though, what was it Will had said? – his dad wasn't too happy about dragging up the past. Yet dragging up the past had almost become a rebirth for her. A chance to start again. It made sense to go back to where she had left off as Elaine McCairn. Divide and conquer. Divide her two personas – Elaine for her everyday life, Alana *only* for her pen-name. Conquer her ghosts. Hold her head high in Castle Ridge once more.

However, there was still something lingering – some nagging *feeling* which she couldn't explain. A feeling that had prompted her to not only send her work to her editor and agent, but send copies to Jack. Like some kind of back-up insurance? She had no idea why. Sometimes, one just had to trust one's instincts...

Time to hit the goody bag, and try to close down the mind before it started prowling. Elaine picked up her little bag of sleep medications and carried it with her into the bedroom, absently calculating whether to take just one, or take the whole bloody lot. It had been that kind of a day, week, year. That kind of a life...

Damn, I need a glass of water...

'Hello, Elaine. Long time, no see.'

She froze mid-turn, not wishing to turn any further. That would mean facing the owner of the voice. Her heart banged in her chest as adrenaline flooded her veins.

'Aren't you going to speak to me?' The voice moved out from the darkness behind the bedroom door.

There were not that many people who knew her as Elaine. And there was something familiar about the voice – something about the way he spoke. She slowly turned around.

Despite the dishevelled appearance – matted hair and beard, careworn features, filthy clothes, Elaine recognised the eyes – one green, one hazel. There was only one person that she knew who had eyes like that.

'Steve...' Tense seconds passed while she tried to regulate her breathing. Screaming would be futile. They were in the middle of nowhere – so who would hear her? 'What are you doing here?'

His voice was taut and gravelly from years of being held silent. 'I've always been here, Elaine. I've followed you to the end of the Earth, and back. I never left you. You walked away from me, remember? You gave up on me.'

'So it was you creeping around in the shadows all these years!' she hissed. 'Do you know how much that scared the shit out of me?' She looked at him, searching for the right words. 'For God's sake, Steve – have you forgotten all that we went through after the accident? After almost drowning in accusations, lies and booze! Yes, it was too much – I had to get away!' Tears began welling in her eyes, ready to spill over. 'I couldn't take it any more...'

'And what makes you think that it was any better for me? Look at me, Elaine! I sank to lows that no-one should ever have to. Do I look like someone who has had a successful life?' He held out his hands, displaying years of dirt under his chewed and broken fingernails, then tugged at his matted hair and beard. His weathered, leathery skin was ingrained with dark lines after decades of outdoor life. 'No! I was pushed around, I was ex-communicated. I was flung out of Castle Ridge, too, you know! People in high places made sure that I wasn't welcome.'

Elaine guessed who he meant by "people in high places" – most likely Julie's parents, and the wealthy business-set that they mingled with. The very same people who had made her feel unwelcome in her own town.

Steve took another step forward out of the shadows towards Elaine, causing her to take an automatic step back. Her eyes were wide with fear, her breathing irregular.

'You don't need to be scared of me, my love...' He shook his head and sighed, before gesturing towards his clothes. 'I'm sorry for the way I look. I didn't want you to see me like this. I wanted to look nice for you. But I couldn't get any new clothes...' His eyes began searching hers for some micro-hope of understanding. Of compassion. 'I hoped that you could love me again.'

Elaine gasped, stumbling over her words. 'Lo...Love you again? Steve... I... It's just not...'

He took another step forward. 'All these years, Elaine... All these years, I've never stopped loving you. You've always been my girl.'

In the faint glow from the bedroom lamp, Elaine noticed a sack-cloth bag in the corner near the door – exactly the same type of bag left at the scene of the dead cat. Her stomach filled with butterflies. Steve followed the direction of her eyes towards the bag, and sprang into the corner to grab it.

'It was you! It was you that left the dead cat on the patio!' Her voice rose in pitch, while her breathing became erratic.

'It wasn't dead when I put it in the bag... It must have died after eating the rat poison...'

Elaine endeavoured to hold her bladder muscles for fear of peeing herself. 'Was it you that left the rose, too?'

'Yes, and all the other little things. Anything for my girl...' His odd coloured eyes locked with Elaine's. A deep, intense look, verging on madness. He smiled, revealing stubs of brown teeth. Elaine's gut lurched at the sight before her. This was far from being the Steve that she remembered as a seventeen-year-old. He had been a good-looking, cock-sure youth with a cheeky smile and mismatched eyes. Shoulder-length hair that you wanted to touch. He had a fancy car, and was training to be a mechanic. If anything, she was in awe of him after her own lowly beginnings.

How the tables had turned – a moment in time which had stripped them both of a future together and sent them on very different paths.

'So, I've decided that if I can't have you, then no-one can. You know how it is... All these years I've had to stand by and watch you with other men. Watch you make a new life. I can't take it any more...' He took another step towards Elaine, causing her to stumble backwards onto the bed.

'Steve! No – please...'

Steve seized the opportunity to jump onto her, overpowering her slight frame. He straddled her waist – his weight and stench pinning her down. Elaine bucked beneath him, and tried to fend him off with blows. The little make-up bag of sleeping tablets dropped out of her hand, spilling the contents onto the bed.

He grabbed her by the wrists, until he felt her slacken from the exertion of trying to fight back. It gave him the opportunity to wriggle higher up her torso, and position his knees over her shoulders and the tops of her arms, effectively trapping her beneath him. The weight of his body crushed into her chest, and the stench of stale piss hindered her breathing.

'Please, Steve – let me go!' She could feel her head starting to tighten through lack of oxygen.

'Don't worry, my love. You won't die alone tonight. I'm coming with you! That way, we can always be together. The way it should have been...'

A renewed sense of urgency geared Steve into action. He reached for the cloth bag, and grabbed a handful of rat-poison pellets, then forcefully wrenched open Elaine's mouth. After stuffing them inside with his fingers, he then held her jaw closed until she had to swallow. She began to gag and choke, spluttering out some of the contents.

Her eyes were manic with terror, as Steve once again forced her mouth open and filled it with more pellets. The more she tried to gasp for breath, the more the pellets began to lodge in her throat and block her airway.

He adjusted his position until he was almost kneeling on her chest – she was not getting away from him! Again he reached inside the bag, this time pulling out a bottle of weedkiller – liquid was clearly needed to help wash down the pellets! He forced open her mouth, flooding it with the deadly poison.

If I can't have her, then no-one can...
If I can't have her, then no-one can...
If I can't have her, then no-one can...

He kept playing this mantra over and over in his mind while he fed her with the lethal cocktail.

Much like the cat on the patio, the mix of rat-poison and weedkiller began to invade its unwilling victim. Slowly, her struggles subsided as her brain, starved by the lack of oxygen, began to shut down.

Steve watched her froth and spasm in agony as he sat astride her, her eyes and tongue bulging from asphyxia, as she entered the point of no return. Her pain would soon be his pain.

He calmly watched and waited, fascinated, until Elaine's fragile grasp on life slipped away. 'Goodbye, my love. We'll meet again on the other side. Our life will be better there.'

In his mind's eye, Steve could no longer see the tortured face of the woman that he'd just taken the life of. The years had rolled back to seeing her as his teen sweetheart. His Elaine. He searched inside the cloth bag for the red rose that he had stolen from the garden. Red for love. He looked at her, then suddenly remembered the bouquet of white roses that he'd seen Will bring this evening. No! She deserved to be sent on her way with grace. Steve scuttled down to the kitchen to retrieve the bouquet, and brought it upstairs.

In a gesture of adulation, he adjusted her body, then carefully began to place the white roses around the corpse. White for grace and purity.

It was time to prepare himself for his journey.

He lined up all that he needed: the same lethal cocktail of poisons that he had administered to Elaine, the red rose stolen from the garden… His eyes focused on the little packages strewn around the bed – the little packets of sleeping tablets and sleep aids. He began opening them until he had a generous handful – he would take those first, then the poisons. And one final thing – he reached inside his overcoat for his battered old wallet. A wallet that contained a photograph of him and Elaine, posing beside the XR3i – the beloved car that would write their death sentences. He looked on the back of the photo at the hand-drawn heart containing the words "Steve & Elaine 4-eva".

And soon they would be.

Chapter 33

Dark Shadows

Friday 21st August, 2015

'Have you got everything, love?' Jack called through to Olivia, who was busying herself in the laundry room.

'Be there in a mo'. Just getting some fresh towels.'

Jack carried the cleaning kit to the front door, together with the pack of clean bedding. Today was Alana's last day at the cottage, much to their relief. They were preparing to meet her there to take the keys, then while Olivia was getting the cottage ready for the next booking, Jack was going to take Alana to the railway station. And out of their life, for the time being, at least. The past month had been more stressful than they had anticipated; they were grateful that she'd decided to cut short her stay.

After Alana had reneged on the end of her stay by one week, Olivia had re-opened the Airbnb bookings calendar. And bingo, just like that, a booking came in – a ten-day stay for a family from London, until after the August Bank Holiday. Long-term lets were easy money. Olivia had soon learned to make the Airbnb stays a minimum of three nights so that she wasn't constantly having to clean, and change bedding.

Olivia came through to the hallway with four sets of clean towels. 'I think that's everything. What time is Alana's train?' she asked.

Jack checked his watch. 'She's taking the 13:58 from Buxton to Manchester Piccadilly, so we've got plenty of time to have a final coffee with her before I take her to the station. The next lot of people don't arrive until this evening, so there's no rush to get the cottage ready. Besides, you know how tidy Alana is – I can't imagine having a big mess to clean up.'

He almost jumped out of his skin as the door intercom system buzzed right by his ear.

'Hello...'

'Post Office delivery. Parcel for Mr Adams to sign for.'

'A parcel?' Jack shrugged towards Olivia, who shrugged in response, equally confused. 'Just a moment.' He pressed the door system to open up for the delivery.

'Sign here, please.' The delivery man passed a clipboard to Jack, together with the parcel.

'Funny, I don't remember ordering anything...' Jack took the proffered pen and signed for the package. He absently returned the clipboard, his mind now absorbed in the unexpected delivery.

He looked at Olivia, his brow furrowed.

It was a package from Alana, addressed to him.

'What do you think it could be?' asked Olivia. 'We're going to see her soon – surely she could give the parcel to you then? And why a signed-for delivery?'

'I dunno...' Jack studied the parcel, before carefully opening the brown paper wrapping. His eyes narrowed when he revealed the contents, his brow totally furrowed in puzzlement. 'Manuscripts? Why would Alana send her manuscripts to me?' He walked back into the kitchen, followed by Olivia, and sat at the breakfast island. She sat beside him, equally as curious.

He looked at the first of the two manuscripts – it was the fully edited version of her latest novel, *Brutal Honesty*; the one that she had been working on during her stay. The cover note showed that she had sent a paper copy to Mr J Adams (himself), and digital copies to her agent and editor. The other manuscript was something new.

Strange, she hadn't mentioned that she was writing anything else...

'What is it? What's the other one?' asked Olivia, puzzled.

'It looks like a rough manuscript for another novel. Called *Dark Shadows*. Wow, she was quick at knocking this one out...'

Jack began flicking through the pages, his expression slowly changing from a look of confusion to one of horror with each line he read. 'Shit...'

'Is something wrong?'

'Good God...the red rose...'

'Jack?'

'The cat...the fucking cat's in the story...'

'Jack! Stop, you're scaring me...'

'A dead kid, ghosts, messages from beyond the grave.'

The more he scanned through the manuscript, the more his eyes widened.

'A stalker...' His hands began shaking as he quickly began reading through random pages, until he reached the final chapter.

'No! No way... Alana!' He jumped up from his seat. 'Quick, quick, grab the car keys...'

'Jack, for fuck's sake, will you *PLEASE* tell me what's going on!' screamed Olivia, the panic rising in her voice.

'It's all about her life, and her time at the cottage. She's made it into fiction; all the names have been changed. But it's everything that happened while she was here. She's written it into a book...' He ran for the door, almost knocking over Olivia in his haste.

'And...?' Olivia's pulse raced, sucked in by Jack's panic.

'And? And it ends with the main character overdosing on sleeping pills, for Chrissakes...'

Though it was normally only a ten-minute drive from their house, through the centre of Buxton, and up to the cottage, it felt like the worst minutes of Jack's life. All the traffic lights in town were on red, all the country lanes were slow-going with tractors and tourists. The journey was frustrating, and surreally *slow-mo*. Jack could feel the beads of sweat running down his spine in the August midday heat, dampening the waistband of his slacks and drenching the back of his shirt. Neither spoke a word, each deep in their own thoughts.

Not caring about damaging the soft grass verge in front of the cottage, Jack quickly pulled up the Volvo, and sat for a moment while he endeavoured to regulate his breathing.

Olivia spoke first. 'Do you think we should call the police before we go in? On account of what we've just read?'

'And tell them what?' Jack shook his head. 'As you once said, she's a novelist – writers have a fertile imagination...'

Olivia could clearly see that his hands were shaking as he fumbled for the spare set of cottage keys, unconvinced by his own rationale. He took a deep breath before opening the car door.

Nothing looked out of the ordinary as they walked up the path; the curtains to the front windows were open and not drawn. Jack rapped with the brass knocker, and waited what he considered a normal length of time for someone to come to the door.

They looked at each other. 'Maybe she's in the back garden and hasn't heard the door? Try again,' Olivia urged.

Jack knocked again, this time with more force. Still nothing. He bent down and shouted through the letterbox. No reply.

'I don't like it. I'm going to use the key...'

As they entered the hallway, Jack noticed that Alana's suitcase was already standing by the foot of the stairs, together with her computer bag and holdall.

He cleared his throat, and called out. 'Alana...'

A heavy silence filled the void.

Jack and Olivia looked at each other. Olivia could see the panic in Jack's eyes, and took hold of his hand.

'C'mon, let's take a look around. I bet she's in the garden enjoying the sunshine...'

'Alana...'

But Alana wasn't in the garden. Nor was she in the kitchen or sitting room.

Reluctantly, they headed to the bottom of the stairs.

'I don't like this...' muttered Jack. 'Something's not right... The house feels too quiet.'

'Surely you don't think...'

Jack looked at Olivia, then closed his eyes and shook his head. He took her hand as they ascended upstairs.

Once at the top, they both stood still and listened for any signs of movement.

Nothing.

The light was still on in the bathroom, but again, this was empty.

Olivia wrinkled her nose as she caught the faint traces of a strange odour. 'What's that smell?'

Jack shrugged, then tapped lightly on the master-bedroom door. 'Alana. Alana, are you there?' He cautiously pushed open the door, then closed his eyes, unwilling to look.

Olivia caught sight of Alana first.

'Oh, my God...'

She froze at the threshold, shocked by the figures laid out on the bed. From what she could make out, some kind of fierce struggle had clearly taken place. The bedding was a mess, and an array of crumpled tablet packets and green-brown pellets were strewn everywhere. Alana's body lay prone on her back, her features bloated and contorted. Twenty-four white roses had been carefully, almost ritualistically, placed around her body – a body which had been set with her arms crossed over a single white rose on her chest.

And beside the body of Alana, lay the body of an old tramp; equally contorted in the face, clutching a single red rose and a photograph; a few tablets and an empty weedkiller bottle close by.

Though the scene was gruesome and disturbing, it looked conversely serene.

Olivia motioned Jack away from the bedroom door. 'We'd better call the police...' she whispered.

Epilogue

"I was technically the last one to see Alana – or Elaine as she was known to me – alive.

I was just on my way home from a seminar in Manchester, and as Buxton is nearby, I decided to stop by the cottage to take her some flowers and a little gift. I wanted to say goodbye before she left. Twenty-five white roses – one for each year that had passed since Jon died. They were meant to be symbolic, a sign of peace and remembrance, just as she had left a white rose every year on my brother's grave.

Of course I came under suspicion – my fingerprints were at the cottage, and there was no sign of a forced entry. Don't they normally say that many people innocently let in their killer? It sounds like something from one of her novels! But in this case, the rear security camera had picked up on an old tramp slipping in through the French doors, just as I was leaving. Besides, I could confirm my whereabouts after I went, and the front camera showed the time that I left and never returned.

The police investigation identified him as being the old tramp who had stayed in the barn at the nearby farm. I say "old tramp", for that's what he looked like. But get this – he was Elaine's old boyfriend from the time of the accident which killed my brother. All these years, it looked as though he'd never stopped loving her. She told me that she often felt like she was being watched, but no-one believed her. She was right to trust her instincts. They found some of Alana's books, as well as some of her underwear secreted away among the hay in the barn where he "lived". The police calculate that's where he got the poisons from, too. Anyway, I hope they both found their peace in the afterlife, to compensate for all that real life threw at them. No-one deserved what they'd been through, or to die the way that they did.

Elaine and I talked about many different things that night, chatting like old friends. Although she felt like she was on the edge of another breakdown, she seemed excited about her new book coming out, and had even found time to work on some new stuff. Her time at the cottage had been productive, and had provided lots of new inspiration. She was all packed, ready to head back to Manchester the next day. She was looking forward to getting back to the city. I think the city noise helped to drown out the voices and dark shadows in her mind.

And although short-lived, our new-found friendship had become very special to me. We had a common but tragic bond. I would have loved to share writing inspiration with her, and hoped to introduce her to my dad one day.

Like me, Dad had often wondered who had been leaving the white roses on Jon's grave, although he had a suspicion that it was Elaine – it was the one day of the year when she reverted to her old name. And though he was caught up in his own grief at the time of Jon's death, he often wondered about the welfare of the "kids", as they were back in 1990. He had heard much of the gossip in Castle Ridge and felt sorry for the way they were being talked about at the time. Worse still, he figured out that much of the ill-will originated from my grandmother – she did a fine job of fuelling rumours while chatting with customers in her fruit shop. Then after Mum died, the ill-will and gossip resurfaced, causing a rift between my dad and my maternal grandparents. It was time for us to make a fresh start, so our life moved on, as did Alana's – or Elaine, as she was known back then.

She told me a great deal about her life, both from her younger days, and her life after she moved away from Castle Ridge. How she had reinvented herself and finally found some happiness. But even with all that, she could never fully let go of the past, and the past wouldn't let go of her. It chipped away at her psyche, and at times plunged her into deep depressions. From the way that she was talking, I was even beginning to worry that she would take her own life. She tried so hard to overcome all that life had thrown at her. But at least she had had the realisation that hiding behind a different persona was not really helping. She had been trying to live under a false identity instead of healing her true-self.

So I've now lost two women that were special to me – my mother, and Elaine. Somehow, they never felt "good enough", despite all that they did.

If only they had both realised what truly amazing women they were."

About the Author

Originally from Chesterfield, England, Ann Thorsson now lives on a farm by the sea, nestled under the iconic Snaefells-glacier, in the beautiful West peninsula of Iceland. She shares this idyll with her Icelandic husband, their two bilingual sons and a bilingual Siberian husky.

Ann's debut novel, *Downhill*, is a gritty drama set in the 1980s coal-mining North of England (published 2019; UK Book Publishing).

Gabriel Rutenberg Photography, Iceland

Her second novel, *Dark Dreams*, is a dark and disturbing tale of secrets and lies, with a supernatural twist (published 2020; UK Book Publishing).

She is currently working on a number of other writing projects, including a collection of local stories, and an anthology of poetry – *Sunflowers: a collection of specially chosen words.*

Acknowledgements and Thanks!

My grateful thanks go to the eagle-eyed team of beta-readers: Josie Lale, Christine Boos and Mark Fearn. To my son, Robert Thor, and to my #1 fan, Henriette. Your constructive feedback and suggestions were invaluable!

To Ruth, Jay, and the team at UK Book Publishing, for getting *Dark Shadows* out into the world.

To my dear friend Heather Burns, of Heather Burns Art – for her artistic genius and creativity on the cover-work of *Dark Shadows*.

To Sophie Draper (author of *Cuckoo*, and *Magpie*) for her help with author research questions.

To the kind and generous people of Old Bolsover Pics Facebook group for sharing all their wonderful anecdotes and memories of *Bolsover Feast* – the annual travelling funfair where we spent our pennies and teen-years posing and looking cool! Happy days!

To all those who have supported me along the way with *Downhill*, *Dark Dreams* and *Dark Shadows*.

Research Acknowledgements:

*https://www.chesterfield.gov.uk/explore-chesterfield/museum/
exhibitions/past-exhibitions/the-crooked-spire.aspx*

Storr A (1998) The Essential Jung (Selected Writings) – Harper Press
(London) Kindle Edition.

For more information about Ann Thorsson:

www.annthorsson.com
@ann.thorsson.author
Facebook: https://www.facebook.com/ann.thorsson.author/
Instagram: https://www.instagram.com/ann.thorsson.author/